WINTERS' SUMMER
By
D. Lamar Jackson

D. LAMAR INK BOOKS are published by

D. Lamar Ink, llc
Hayward, CA 94544
info@dlamarink.com
www.dlamarink.com

ISBN-13: 978-0985459536
ISBN-10: 0985459530

D. LAMAR INK. LLC

DEDICATION

This Book is dedicated to both of my parents, Ellis and Stephanie Jackson. Mom, you were the first to tell me to write my ideas down on paper and see where it takes me. Pop, you have been my biggest supporter and I love you for it.

Chapter 1

Sean Winters

Time always seems to stop here. My world begins to make sense and all the world's troubles are gone. Here, I am where I should be. I am where I want to be. I am where I have to be. I make the rules. I have the final say. Here, I am boss, I am king, I am in control. Here, I make time stand still if only for a moment. Frame by frame, I capture what some would say is worth a thousand words. Here, I expose people for who they are. Here, I fix the world's flaws and imperfections. Here, I make the ordinary extraordinary.

Okay, I may be feeling myself just a bit much. But, if you had the life I have you would be cocky too. I mean I'm good, I'm great, I'm the best and no one can tell me otherwise. At twenty-eight years old I am on top of my game. Better yet,

I'm ahead of the game. I'm making more money than both my parents combined. I'm living in a nice condo and driving this years S Class Benz; not to mention I'm sleeping with a model.

That's just a snapshot of my life; I'll explain more later. Right now I have to get on my grind and make some magic happen. I'm an artist, digital, but an artist still the same. I take a rough canvas and I turn it into the photos you see in Essence, Jet, Ebony and Hair Magazine. I take a regular person and turn them into what you see on club flyers, bus benches and even billboards. At this moment Alexis is my canvas.

At times, it's a hard job. Thank God for Adobe photo shop. Everyone seems to have some type of flaw I have to fix to make them look like the people we all strive to be. I mean I have to take out moles, put in a mole, eradicate pimples, widen butts, bust, hips and lips. I was beginning to think no one was perfect until I met this women here in front of me. Alexis Washington, God's Mona Lisa, His perfect canvas.

The shot is set. Miles, my assistant, has the lights in perfect position. Melanie, a photographer and make-up artist, works flawlessly as usual. The set is perfect. A white chaise lounge with purple sheets draped over the back sits against a green screen. A half eaten box of chocolates sits in front of the lounge with red roses scattered on the floor. Alexis sits on the lounge with her legs curved under her and a glass of red wine in her hand. Here is my vision of the perfect welcome home for a new magazine B. L. A C. K.

Alexis smiles for the camera wearing nothing but a pink tank top and matching boy shorts. Her smile brightens my day, like the sun when it rises over the hills in my hometown of Oakland, California. She is hella fine, from her straight brown hair to her big brown eyes and her soft brown lips shimmering with earth tone lip-gloss. She stands five foot ten and about a hundred and twenty-five pounds with perfect curves. I am her photographer. I am her friend. I am her man. I am the one she comes home to.

We met two years ago when she came to my photography studio, A Moment in Time, to get head shots.

She was new to LA and wanted to
get into dancing. I remember it like
it was yesterday. She had on little
make up, strawberry lip-gloss and
eye shadow. I had been in LA for
two years and had never seen a
woman that looked as good as Alexis
without much make-up. She wore
a silver chain around her neck with
a silver cross dangling from it. It
reminded me of my childhood and
how far removed I was from the
church and the nickname P. K.,
Preachers Kid.

 "I'm a professional dancer," she
told me when I asked what brought
her in.

 I almost couldn't speak to her.
This had only happened to me once
before. Normally I'm pretty smooth
and my conversation game is
seamless. But with Alexis I was
speechless, even though she was
like a breath of fresh air.

 "My, my, name is Shh, shh,
Sean." She was so beautiful that I
stumbled over my words the entire
shoot. She giggled at me a bit. She
knew she made me a little nervous.
I knew from there I didn't stand a
chance. A woman wants a man
with confidence and who is sure of
himself. At that moment, I was like

a kid in high school trying to ask a girl I liked to go with me.

"You know you should think about being a model," I told her at the end of the shoot. "I have a friend who's an agent that is looking for a girl like you."

Alexis rolled her eyes. "Look, shh, shh, Sean, if you want to ask me out just ask. I am not going to be impressed by the fact you may or may not know an agent and I'm not going to jump into bed with you because I think you're going to help advance my career. Now you're a good looking guy and shouldn't be nervous about asking me out. But if you're going to start off by lying, then don't bother asking me out and just let me know how much I owe you and when I can pick up my head shots."

Her little tangent made me a little scared but at the same time turned me on. It's good to see a black woman be so sure of herself. Just like a woman needs a confident man, a man needs a confident woman. A woman who isn't confident in herself is a woman walking around with a big sign that says use me and abuse me.

I tried to regain my composure and get my swag back. "Okay Ms. Alexis, do you want to go out Friday?"

"Sorry I'm busy."

My mouth dropped; I couldn't believe she just played me. I had fallen in and out of love in less than a minute.

Alexis walks towards the exit door, stops and turns around. "I am free on Saturday."

My strength was renewed and my attraction to Alexis even stronger. What else could I say? "Saturday at seven then?"

"You have my number on the paper work I filled out." She smiles and exits.

I immediately got on the phone and called my agent friend, Maria. Even though Alexis didn't believe I had a friend who was an agent, I did. We went to Cal State East Bay together where she majored in Theatre. Maria, who was my very first customer, had me do her headshots when we were still in school. She came to LA about a year before me and started working at a talent agency while looking for acting jobs. She became an agent and started sending all of her talent

9

to me when I touched down in LA. If it wasn't for Maria, I probably wouldn't be as successful as I am now. It's because of her I am contracted with her agency and five other agencies in LA. Plus, a lot of new talent that comes to town looking for headshots are recommended to come to me.

"Hey, Maria, I have just seen a girl that you may want to work with."

"Really?" Maria says, "And since when do you refer people to me?"

"Since this firecracker just changed my life. She's a dancer but she has the look of a model without even trying."

"Okay, well if you think she's good, have her meet me on Monday morning at ten."

"I will."

I hang up the phone and pat myself on the back.

That Saturday I took Alexis out to dinner and on a walk along Santa Monica Beach. We had a good time, shared our meals, held hands and joked a lot. When I dropped her off at home, she informed me that she doesn't kiss guys on the first date. This is when I told her about Maria and her wanting to meet her on Monday. At first she didn't believe me, so I gave her the address, time and phone number to Maria's agency. After that, Alexis broke her rule of not kissing on the first date. This wouldn't be the last time we broke a rule.

Alexis met with Maria and it didn't take long before she landed her first print ad. That was two years ago and Alexis has stayed on her grind. She has been in several print ads and music videos. The last one had her away from me for a few weeks. It made me realize that I loved her. Even though I had said it after only three months of dating, I didn't really mean it until she was away. I decided to buy a ring and I have just been waiting for the right time to give it to her. Maybe I'll ask her this weekend when I take her up to Oakland to visit my parents and celebrate my father's church anniversary.

Alexis walks over to me, her golden brown skin shinning from the sweat and make-up. She smiles and my heart melts. Her big brown eyes put me in a trance. The shoot is over and it's time to pack up but I can't move because I am still so mesmerized by her beauty.

"You ready to go home?" Alexis asks, in the sweetest voice. She pulls on one of the middle buttons of my tan shirt. I can tell she's feeling hot. She tells me all the time that she wants me more when I'm taking her picture than any other time. Something about our photo shoots is so sexy to her that she has to remind herself that she's working. I have to do the same.

"We can go in minute. You can go to the office and change."

"How about I just put my sweat suit on but leave what I have on for you?"

"You have some stuff at home similar." I remind her.

Alexis feels the fabric of the underwear, her small hands caressing her skin. "I don't have anything this nice."

I look at her and smile. At this moment I'm happy. Not because Alexis is half naked, not because of the way she feels on the fabric, not because she is beautiful. I am happy because she is mine and all mine.

"I will buy you some for your birthday."

She smiles and kisses me softly on the lips. Her strawberry lip-gloss tastes so sweet. Her soft tongue finds it's way into my mouth. I massage her tongue with mine as I put my hands on her hips.

"Get a room," Melanie says as she walks past us."

Alexis and I come back to reality as our moment of passion is interrupted. Alexis smiles at me. "I'll be in the office changing." Alexis walks away from me and I can't tell which is more sexy, her walk towards me or her walk away from me. Either way I enjoy watching her walk.

I look around at Miles and Melanie who are cleaning up. "Alright guys! Good job today! Let's get cleaned up and go home."

They give half cheers and fake smiles. They're tired and have been up doing photo shoots for the past twelve hours. I've shot four girls today for three different magazines. I had to squeeze them all in today because I will be gone for the next three days visiting my parents. My crew is good though and don't mind putting in the long hours, especially if it means they'll get a three day weekend out of it.

Miles walks over to me. "Hey Sean, can I ask you a question?"

Miles is a cool dude. Fresh out of college with a bright future ahead of him. He stands about two inches shorter than me at about 6 foot and keeps his hair and beard wild and natural. He's my right hand man and an aspiring photographer in his own right.

"What's up Miles?"

"I know we're supposed to be off the next three days but I was wondering if I could use the studio this weekend?"

I look at Miles, thinking I can't believe this Negro. This light skinned, green-eyed cat really wants me to hand over the keys to my studio? I mean he's a great assistant but I've only known him for about six months. We're cool but I don't know if we're that cool just yet.

"I don't let anybody use my studio when I'm away. What are you trying to do?"

"Just trying to sharpen my skills. I'll bring my wife in and just take some shots and of her."

Wife? Since when was this young kid married? I thought he was only twenty-two. What is he doing married already? He must have knocked this girl up or something. I mean that's the only reason most folks get married nowadays anyway, especially at that young of an age. At twenty-two, I was jumping in and out bed with so many different women it was crazy. I wasn't thinking about marriage, not until Alexis.

"When were you going to tell me you were married?"

Miles looks as if he just put his foot in his mouth. "I guess it just never came up. Wasn't anything personal."

Melanie walks over, "I just found out today when he showed me a picture. I told him I would come in with him so you don't have to worry.

Melanie is a beautiful thick, chocolate sista with a good heart and great sense of humor. I've known her since my college days. In fact, we dated for about two-minutes our sophomore year. She's the only one that understood my on again, off again relationship with Summer Boyd, my childhood sweetheart. All Melanie wanted was honesty and she was honest with me. I wasn't the only guy she dated. At first I was cool with it, because she was sexy, but after finding out she slept with some of the other guys she dated, I had to let that go.

We stayed friends throughout school. She stayed behind an extra year because she got pregnant and needed to take a couple of quarters off. Now before you judge, I want to make it clear; she was not a hoe, but a woman, who like me, was exploring all her options. When she got pregnant, she was actually a senior and in a committed relationship with a musician named Paul Rock. After college, they got married and moved to LA where she started working with me while he got a gig playing drums for an R&B group. Over the past two years, Paul or P. Rock as he is called has been making a name for himself by writing and producing songs for other artists in the business.

I take my studio key off my key chain and hand it to Melanie. "If you're both going to be here, then I guess that's okay, but I'm not paying you guys for this time."

Miles shakes my hand. "Thanks, Sean, I appreciate it."

Melanie pats me on the shoulder, "See, there is a heart

inside that bird chest of yours after all."

Miles laughs an uncomfortable laugh.

I pound my chest with a closed fist, "It hasn't been a bird chest since I was twelve."

"Delusional." Melanie laughs as she walks away.

I look Miles in the eye with all seriousness," Don't mess up my studio."

Miles looks back into my eyes, "I won't."

I walk to the front of the of the studio as my phone rings. I pull the phone from the belt clip and look at the caller ID. It's Natalie, one of my childhood friends and an up and coming fashion designer. I answer.

"Hey Natalie, what's going on, Sis?"

"Nothing much baby boy. What's new with you?"

"Same old thing. Taking pictures of beautiful women all day."

"Getting paid to be a peeping Tom. Your dream job." Natalie has always been sarcastic.

"Whatever Nat, what up?"

"Just making sure you and the model are coming to the opening of my store Saturday night. "

I shake my head. Natalie knows Alexis' name but never uses it. Being that Natalie has done several fashion shows and has worked with a number of models, she has come to the conclusion that all models are dumb or too into themselves. Natalie doesn't know Alexis but has already pre-judged her based on her profession.

"Alexis and I will be there."

"Good, I want to meet this girl you are so crazy about."

I try to change the subject.

"Is Summer going to be there?"

Natalie takes a long breath. I knew I shouldn't have asked the question but at the same time I really wanted to know.

"Yes, she'll be there, Sean."

I feel myself getting excited and nervous at the same time. Summer Boyd, my first love, my first everything. I haven't seen Summer in two years. The last time I saw her, I left her sitting in my condo. I wanted her to stay. She had other plans. She was about to become a pediatrician in Oakland. My photography business was growing in LA. I wanted to be with Summer more than anything; we just could never make it work. She was always meeting some new guy up in Oakland and I had a variety of women coming to my studio willing to do anything for a discount on their headshots. Summer has still always stayed on my mind and now I'm going to see her this weekend.

"Sean, I don't want you ruining this day for me okay. You and Summer broke up a long time ago; you both are dating other people so don't go bringing up the past."

Natalie was right, the past is the past but I still had feelings for Summer. We talked on the phone a few times after she left the last time. We still cared for one another, it was obvious in our conversations. What I wouldn't give to be with her one last time. To kiss her lips, to hold her in my arms, to smell her intoxicating perfume.

"I promise I won't start anything, but you better tell Summer the same."

"Boy please! You better get a clue, Summer was over you the day she left you in LA. She had a date the day she came back. Sorry baby but you're the one I'm worried about."

I'm doubly shocked. I thought Summer would have least waited a week or two before going out with a new guy. And Natalie thinks I'm the one who she needs to worry about? She must not know her friend as well as she thinks; Summer could be quite the aggressor at times. Me on the other hand, I could sleep with a girl one night and act like I don't know her the next. Even though Summer isn't the average girl, I have a woman so Natalie need not worry about me. On the other hand, if me and Summer were to be alone together, who knows what would happen?

"Look, I'll be on my best behavior, okay?"

"You better because this day is very important to me and I don't want to have to beat you up. And before you say anything just remember I beat you up in high school and I can beat you up now."

"Now you know that was a sucker punch, you caught me off guard."

I remember accidentally spilling soda all over one of Natalie's designs. I told her to just draw another picture and the next thing I can remember is being on the ground and my friend Eric pulling Natalie off of me.

"Yea, yea, just be a good boy."

"I will. See you tomorrow."

I hang up the phone and walk into my office. Alexis sits on the edge of my mahogany wood desk.

"You ready?" She says in that soft sweet voice of hers.

She sits there with a powder blue sweat suit on with a pink top showing from her half zipped sweater jacket. Her skin still glows although the water bottle in her hand has helped her cool off a bit. She has a black gym bag on one of her shoulders and a small purse on the other.

"Sure we can go. Melanie can lock up."

Alexis looks a little confused, "You gave Melanie a key to the studio?"

Alexis knows all about Melanie and our past and she's not jealous because she knows it was never serious. I've always been honest when in a relationship, so Alexis knows about the three different models I slept with before her and she even knows about Summer.

"I gave her my key. She and Miles are coming in to do a shoot off the clock."

"Good, because I am tired and want to get some sleep before our long drive tomorrow."

We walk out of the building and towards my sapphire blue Benz. It took a lot of hard work to get this car and I take extra special care of it. Other than my condo, it's the most important purchase I've made. It's my baby. It took almost a year before I let Alexis drive my car to a dance class one day because her car was in the shop. I called her every twenty minutes to check on the car like I was a new parent leaving my kid with the baby-sitter for the first time.

"It's only about six hours and besides you'll probably be sleep the whole time anyway. There is no way I'm letting you drive."

She playfully hits me in the stomach.

"What's that supposed to mean? You trying to tell me I can't drive?"

"Let's just say you drive like you live in LA."

Alexis rolls her eyes and gets in on the passenger side. I get in the driver's seat, press start and drive off.

Alexis yawns and stretches. "I am not doing this again. Teaching three dance classes then coming to do a photo shoot. I must have been out of my mind."

"We needed to get the photo shoot done this weekend. You knew we were going to be out of town for a few days."

I see her look at me from the corner of my eye. "Speaking of being out of town, is your girlfriend going to be in town this weekend?"

I pretend as if I don't know who she's talking about. "You're my girlfriend."

"You know who I'm talking about. What's her name? Oh yeah, Fall."

"Summer." I fell right into that one.

"That's right, Summer." She laughs.

In an effort to be completely open to Alexis, I told her all about Summer. I told her how Summer was my first love, my first everything. Alexis has never met Summer but knows her like her sister. Alexis even knows how Summer and I split apart or grew apart or fell apart.

"Summer may be there; I'm not sure." I say trying not to smile.

I don't know why I lied. I knew Summer would be around and that I was going to run into her at some point. Maybe I want to protect Alexis' feelings. She's told me how she's been cheated on by every boyfriend she's ever had until me. I know she can be insecure and have a hard time trusting. I especially know she doesn't trust other women because she's been burned by some so called good friends. I try not to mention Summer around Alexis because even though they've never met, Alexis is jealous of Summer.

"Oh please. I know she's going to be there. Natalie is opening her own clothing store. Of course Summer is going to be there to support her best friend."

I just nod.

Alexis stares at me for a few moments trying to get a reaction out of me. I concentrate extra hard trying not give her one.

"So, what are you going to say to her when you see her?"

I pretend she's talking about Natalie.

"Well, I'm going to tell Natalie I'm proud of her and wish her success in her business."

Alexis slaps me on the arm with an open hand. "You know that's not who I meant, Sean."

I know now that I have to be reassuring. I have to think of something to say that will let Alexis know I love her and want to be with her. "Look, if I see Summer, I'm going to just ask her how she is and that's that."

"And what if she tells you that she misses you and wants you back?"

At first she was trying to get a reaction out of me but now Alexis is letting jealousy take over. We stop at a red light. I look Alexis in her eyes. "I will tell her that she's too late, I already have a good woman."

Alexis kisses me. The light turns green and I drive off. Alexis turns her head towards the window and closes her eyes. She's trying to get a little nap even though we should be home within twenty minutes.

I hope what I told her was sufficient enough to put her mind at ease. But the truth is I don't know what I would say to Summer if she told me she wanted me back. It's been two years since we had been together. Two years since I held her in my arms. Two years since I kissed her soft, pink lips. Two years since we made love. Two years since I said I love you and heard her say I love you back.

I remember the first time I saw her. It was the end of summer in North Oakland, on 44th and Market, the fifth house on the block. I was a skinny twelve-year-old kid and was just beginning to become interested in the opposite sex. I remember sitting on the stairs that led to my two-story house listening to a little hip-hop on my boom box stereo. I heard my mom talking about how the new neighbors were moving into the house across the street from us that day so I wanted to be the first to see the new folks on the block.

I didn't know much about the couple that lived in the house before. My mother said the husband couldn't keep his hands off of his wife. I remember the police showing up at the house on several different occasions, a few times taking the husband away. The wife would cry as the police car drove away with her husband in the back seat. Things would seem normal for a day or two, then the husband always came back home and within a week the police were called again. A few months earlier the police and ambulance came, I saw the husband sitting in the back of the police car as usual but this time the wife wasn't crying for him. This time the wife was on a stretcher being put inside the ambulance. I never saw her or her husband again. A few weeks later the house was up for sale and sold quickly.

I watch as a grey Toyota sedan pulls into the driveway. A tall light skinned man gets out and stretches. A few seconds later, a beige mini van pulls into the driveway. The side doors open and two girls get out. One is about my age and the other a few years younger. Their mother gets out of the driver seat of the car and smiles at her new home. A giant moving van pulls up and parks on the street. Except for a few brief moments, my eyes never leave the first girl to hop out of the minivan.

"What up, yo?" My best friend and neighbor Eric Reed rides up to the front porch on his 10-speed bicycle. He breaks my trance, my

27

thoughts, and my prepubescent fantasies. He wears coveralls with one of the pant legs rolled up. He also has on an Oakland A's cap backwards.

"What's up, Homie?" I say without looking at him. At least that's what I think I said. My eyes stay locked on the girl across the street.

Eric puts the kickstand out and lets his bike rest in front of my house. He walks up and stands next to me on my red porch.

"So I see the new people is moving in. Think they know a woman got killed in there a few months ago." Eric always liked to point out the negative in every situation. I don't know why but he can never see the positive.

Natalie, another neighbor and good friend, walks up to my porch and stands on the stair above Eric, making her look a little taller. "What's up Sean and Loser?" Natalie is always so cheerful and full of life, but she will talk about you in a second.

I greet Natalie but Eric takes a step further.

"Loser! You calling me a loser and you wearing the same outfit you were wearing yesterday?"

Natalie can always be seen in a pair of blue jeans and a black top and black headband.

"Man, I don't know. If they do know, they don't look like they care. And if they don't know don't mean they need to know." I finally answer Eric's question.

"I'ma go tell them." Eric says.

Natalie slaps Eric on the back of the head, almost knocking off his coke bottle glasses. Eric rubs the back of his head. Natalie grabs Eric by the arm and turns him to face her. "Don't do that. They don't need to know about that lady getting killed in their new house."

Eric tries to justify his reasons. "Why not? I would want to know if my new house might be haunted."

I stand. "The house isn't haunted. She's fine. I mean they're fine."

Natalie pops me on the shoulder. "You like the girl over there, don't you?"

I rub my shoulder and try to hide my true feelings. "No, I don't even know her."

Eric and Natalie look at each other and I can tell that they are thinking the same thing.

Eric speaks first. "Well, lets introduce you."

Eric and Natalie start heading towards the new neighbors. I try to get them to stop but once they have their minds set on something, they do it. I finally give up and walk slowly behind them. We all look both ways before crossing the street. As we walked up the short driveway, we see the mother taking the younger girl into the house. The older girl stands at the mini van and tries to help her father with a box. She turns to see us walking towards her and looks a little worried and scared.

"Daddy," she says in an almost whisper.

Her Father stops doing what he's doing and looks at us, probably thinking who are these three hoodlums walking up his driveway.

"Are you three the welcoming committee?" He asks in a strong deep voice.

Eric is the first to blurt something out. "We just wanted to let you know that your house may be haunted because a lady got..."

Natalie covers Eric's mouth to silence him. "We were just coming over to say hello."

"Well, hello. My name is Dr. Thomas Boyd." Dr. Boyd reaches his hand out for one of us to shake it.

Eric pulls Natalie's hand from his mouth and shakes Dr. Boyd's hand.

"My name is Eric, but everybody calls me Eazy Money, because I make making money look easy."

"Nice to meet you, but I think I'll call you Eric."

Natalie shakes Dr. Boyd's hand next. "My name is Natalie, future fashion designer, and I'm the smart one in this group."

I shake Dr. Boyd's hand last but I still have my eyes fixed on Dr. Boyd's daughter who's giving me that shy girl smile and keeps looking away.

"My name is Sean. I live right across the street."

Dr. Boyd smiles and nods his head. "I saw you on your porch checking us out." He takes his hands and brings his daughter close to him. "This is my oldest daughter Summer. My youngest, Nicole, just went into the house with her mother."

Summer waves at us. "Hi."

Dr. Boyd takes the box from Summer. "Why don't I help your mother inside while you stay out here and make some new friends."

"Okay, Daddy."

Dr. Boyd takes the box and walks into the house. Eric walks up to Summer.

"Did you know a woman got killed here a few months ago?"

Summer gets a little nervous and begins to back up. Natalie slaps Eric in the back of the head. She takes Summers hand as Eric rubs his head.

"Don't mind him, Summer, your house is not haunted or anything."

"You sure?"

I walk up to Summer. "We're sure. But if you have any problems you can always come across the street to my place and I'll protect you."

Summer looks at me. Our eyes finally lock on each other for longer than a few seconds. "You promise?"

"Cross my heart and hope to die," I say as I actually make a cross on my chest with my finger.

I smile at her. She smiles back. This was the beginning of a life-long love affair with the two of us. Well, at least a twelve-year affair. We shared a lot together over the years. Our first kiss, our first date, our first dance and even our first sexual experience. Even when we weren't together, we were always there for each other. When she left me, I didn't think I could ever love again until I met Alexis. Now, after two years, I think I'm ready to marry Alexis.

I pull into the garage of my two story Condo and park. I look over at Alexis who has been asleep the whole car ride home. She is such a good woman. I feel bad sometimes because I compare her to Summer a lot. I've compared every woman to Summer, which is probably why none of my relationships last; but I'm determined to make this one last. It's not like I'm getting any younger. Not saying twenty-eight is old, but I thought I'd be married by now. The thing is, I thought I'd be married to Summer.

I take my hand and run my fingers softly through Alexis' soft brown hair. She stirs a little. She looks so beautiful when she's asleep. I smile at her as she rubs her nose. She then opens her eyes as she notices that the engine has stopped running.

"We're home already?" She must have really been tired if she fell into such a deep sleep. I know the days she teaches dance are exhausting but with the photo shoot tonight, she's probably beyond tired.

"Yeah, just got here."

Alexis stretches her arms and neck. She sneezes twice into her arm trying not spread any germs. She reaches for the glove box. "Do you have some tissues in here? My nose is running."

I try to stop before she opens the glove box and finds my surprise, but I'm too slow. Alexis is stunned and motionless as she sees the tiny black ring box in my glove box. She puts one hand on her chest and the other over mouth. She looks at me, her eyes filled with tears, but not flowing down her cheek. I smile at her, that's all I can do now that the secret's out. She reaches for the box and slowly takes it out of the glove box. Her hands shake as she opens the box and finds a two-karat, princess cut, diamond engagement ring.

"Is this what I think it is?" He voice shaky as she tries to fight back tears. She looks at me and that's when a tear comes down the side of her face.

"I was going to wait until this weekend to ask you."

"Ask me what?" As if she didn't know.

"We've been together these past two years and I feel we should take it to the next level. So, Alexis Rene Washington, will you marry me?"

Alexis smiles through a flowing stream of tears. She nods and gives me a yes. She leans over and gives me a long kiss. I then take the ring and slide it on to her ring finger.

"Come on, Sean, let's go inside to celebrate."

Alexis gets out of the car and heads for the door that leads to the house. She stops and looks back at me as I sit behind the wheel of my car. She smiles and I smile back. I can't believe I'm engaged now and to Alexis. This wasn't my plan. I wanted to wait until Sunday before coming home to ask Alexis to marry me. That would give me enough to time to see Summer, see if there was something still there for us. I want to make sure it's actually over with

us or if we should be together. I
don't want to hurt Alexis but I know
I can't marry her unless I know how
Summer feels about me. Summer
may have left me but I know she
still loves me. But does she love me
enough to get back with me? As I
look at Alexis standing by the door,
I'm starting to think that I have
made a big mistake.

Chapter 2

Alexis Washington

I walk into the two-bedroom condo feeling like I'm in a fairy tale. After all of the heartache and pain I have endured over my entire life, I'm finally happy. At twenty-six years old I've lived a life that some sixty-two year old women couldn't imagine. Until I met Sean, I thought my life was all about losing. Losing my mother eight years ago. Losing my big sister to a man who married and moved her to Atlanta. Losing my little brother to the street life and eventually to jail. Losing boyfriend after boyfriend. Losing job after job with no real direction.

The two things that make life worth living for me are love for God and my love for dancing. It was my mother who made me go to church every Sunday with the neighbors because she had to work. She would read the Bible to me every

night before I went to bed and
taught me that no matter what my
situation, God is there protecting
me, loving me and caring for me. I
miss my mother more than anything
but I take comfort in knowing she's
in heaven with God and doesn't
have to deal with the stress of life
anymore.

I deal with the stress of life
through dance. I first fell in love
with dancing when I joined the
praise team at my church in
Chicago, Illinois. Whenever I did a
praise dance, I felt closer to God.
My love for dance then branched out
when I found a dancing school near
my home. My mother, always
supportive, found a way for me to
take the classes. I got so good that
by the time I was fourteen, I was
teaching two dance classes on
Saturdays. I dreamed I would be
able to go to Hollywood and become
a famous choreographer and create
dance moves for music videos and
movies. Little did I know all of my
dreams would come true and then
some.

I toss my gym bag on the couch
and walk up the stairs. I go to the
washer and dryer, which is right
next to the stairs and across from

the master bedroom. As I take a load out of the washer and put it in the dryer I finally hear Sean walk in the door. I wonder what's going through his mind as I start the dryer and proceed to take a load of dirty clothes and put them into the washer.

I have been waiting on Sean to propose for over a year now. I knew he was a good guy from the moment we met. Even though Sean was obviously nervous around me, I could see he had a good heart. When I walked into to his studio to get head shots I had no idea I would be meeting my future husband. I was fresh out of a two-year relationship with a drug dealer named Keith who helped usher my little brother James into the life. He was physically and emotionally abusive, but he kept me in nice cars and expensive clothes. But after my brother went to jail, I saw that the life I was in wasn't for me. So, I left him and Chicago in search of a dancing career. A few weeks later my ex was arrested. My brother gave him up in order to receive a lighter sentence. Now James will be getting out next year, hopefully in time for my wedding. Keith is serving ten. James has found God and tells me that he wants to be a minister when he gets out. I'm hoping he comes to Los Angeles with me when he gets out. I don't want him in Chicago when Keith gets out. Keith and Sean are like night and day. Had I stayed in Chicago, I never would have met Sean.

I remember the day I met Sean vividly. I had been in Los Angels for a little over a year. I was getting nowhere fast. I went on audition after audition and couldn't get a job because I didn't have a resume or headshots. A girl I met at several auditions told me where she got her headshots done and told me the photographer was good and fine. I decided to go to Sean's studio, A Moment in Time. I knew right off the back that if Sean asked me out it wouldn't be long before we slept with each other. I was trying to be good. I made the mistake of sleeping with a guy before really knowing him and then finding out it was a big mistake. With Sean, I didn't want to make that same mistake.

Sean stood about six-foot-one and had beautiful milk chocolate skin. I noticed his narrow brown eyes that looked honest. No facial hair, so I got full view of his thick chocolate lips that begged to be kissed. He kept licking them, which made me think about him licking me. He was dressed casual in a pair of dark denim jeans with a brown button down shirt and brown dress shoes. I was in love with him before he even spoke. But he almost blew it when he spoke. His stuttering was cute and I wanted to get to know him better. Much better.

Sean was a perfect gentleman. He was smart, funny, and most of all good looking. But what Sean had that all of my past boyfriends didn't have was a loyal spirit about him. I could tell that no matter what, Sean wouldn't cheat on me like all of my boyfriends in the past have. I learned that by seeing how long he could wait before having sex or pressuring me to have sex. Sean never pressured me or made it seem that he could have any woman he wants, and right now he wants me, so I better get with it or miss out. Truth is, I came close to sleeping with Sean on our first date when I found out he got me a meeting with an agent. But I held back and only kissed him. For weeks I had to fight the urge to give it up to Sean every time we were together. It was probably harder for me to hold back than it was for him, or at least it seemed that way.

"Sean, you gonna take a shower?" I call down to him. He still hadn't made his way up the stairs.

" Yeah, I'll be up in a minute," he replies.

I turn on the washing machine and walk into the bedroom. I sit on the bed and look at my ring in amazement. I still can't believe I'm actually getting married. The sad thing is I don't know who to call first. I could call my sister but the two of us have never really been close. She's always been into herself and in her own world. She would always act as if the world owed her something because she was born. I just could never be that self-centered, not when God is my center.

I think about my Aunt and cousins that live in LA. Aunt Gloria, my mother's younger sister, would be happy. I look at the time and decide to call her in the morning because it's pretty late and my aunt has to be to work early in the morning. I decide to call my cousin

Simone, who is Aunt Gloria's oldest
daughter and my former roommate
when I moved from Chicago. I take
my cell phone from my jacket pocket
and dial Simone's number.

Simone answers by the third
ring. "What's up, Cuz?"

"Guess what, Monie?"

"Girl, it is too late to be playing
the guessing game. You better spit
it out or tell it to dial tone." Simone
snaps back.

"Sean finally did it." I say as
Sean walks into the bedroom, taking
off his shirt and showing off his
toned body as he walks to the
closet. The site of Sean's body
makes me moist. I love that my
man stays in shape. With my
working out all the time to stay fit, I
couldn't be with someone who didn't
take the same care with their body.

"What, he proposed to you?"
Simone says with a bit of sarcasm.

"Yes, Girl, I'm getting married."

Simone and I scream like little
teenage girls. I go over all of the
details about how I found the ring
and then Sean proposing. Sean
walks out of the closet, shakes his
head and smiles at me. He walks to
the bathroom and closes the door,
which signals that he has to do

number two before taking his shower. Otherwise he would leave the door open so I can get a little show while he bathed himself.

"So girl, we are going to get to planning as soon as you come back from Oakland?" Simone says with more excitement than I could have imagined.

Simone is about a year younger than me and has a son, Daniel, whom I grew close to while we were sharing an apartment in NoHo. Simone helped me get used to the LA life and we have been like best friends ever since. We saw each other every once in a while when we were kids, but never really got to spend time together like we did when I came from Chicago.

"You know you're going to be my maid of honor, right?"

"You would want me to be. I would have to disown you if I wasn't," Simone says with a laugh.

"Alright, Monie, let me get off this phone and get to bed. We have a long drive tomorrow. I'll call you later though."

"Okay, love you, Cuz."

"Love you too." I say as I end the call.

I could have never imagined
that I would be in a ton of print ads,
choreographing musicals and
videos, teaching several dance
classes and getting married to a
great photographer. I've only been
in LA for three years but my life has
done a complete one-eighty and I
am happy everyday. I just pray this
joy never ends.

I get down on my knees and
instead of just praying I praise God
for all the wonderful things He's
done in my life. I thank Him for
taking me from one extreme to
another. At one point in my life, I
had no faith in love, but now, I
believe in love. As I finish my
praise, I hear the toilet flush then
the shower begins to run. I pray the
joy I have right now is never taken
away.

As I begin to fold the clothes I
took out of the dryer, I pick up a
pair of boy shorts Sean bought me
for his birthday last month. He says
he loves to see me in them,
especially when I'm just walking
around the house. It makes me
think if Sean had ever bought boy
shorts for any other women. Has he
ever bought some for Summer, his
first love? I've never been insecure,

but knowing that Summer will be in Oakland this weekend makes me feel uncomfortable.

I know all about Sean's past relationship with Summer. Summer seems to be the only woman who he has never gotten over. I know we will run into her this weekend at Natalie's grand opening of her store. I'm not sure how I feel about meeting Summer for the first time. I wonder how Sean will act when he sees Summer. Are old feeling going to resurface? Will he think he made a mistake by proposing to me tonight? I then begin to wonder if that's why Sean said he was planning to wait until the end of the weekend to propose to me? Does he want to have one last fling with Summer before walking down the aisle?

I look at my ring long and hard. I will give him the ring back if he cheats, but I really don't want to give it back. It's so beautiful. It's what I've always wanted. It's my ring. So Sean better keep it in his pants this weekend and forever if he wants to marry me. Summer shouldn't even be an option. The problem, however, is that Summer is an option.

Chapter 3

Sean

I hop out the shower hoping I have washed away all the negative thoughts swimming through my mind. I'm trying to get back to myself. I'm never unsure about anything. I'm always in control. But when it comes to love, I have no say. How dare love make me second-guess myself! I have been with Alexis for two years now. We have loved and have made love. There should be no doubt that I have come to the right decision. She is the one for me.

I grab my towel and dry off, while I look in the mirror and see the man I have become. Not a hypocrite like my father, The Good Reverend Winters. I've become successful and I did it all on my own. I'm bringing in anywhere from ten to fifteen thousand dollars a month taking pictures while my father is praying hard every day that his congregation will grow again.

I'm nothing like The Good Reverend Winters; I'm a good man and would never put Alexis through what my father put my mother through. The humiliation, the embarrassment, the hurt and the pain. So I have to leave Summer in the past so that she doesn't ruin my future.

I step out of the bathroom and see Alexis sitting on the bed wearing nothing but a smile. Her body is perfect to me. Long, smooth neck, perfect C-cup breasts, toned ABS, long legs and a nice perfectly toned ass. She has a dancer's body, very slim but curvy. She stretches her arms in the air and yawns. I feel like giving her the business right now.

"It's about time, Mr. Winters. I was about to fall asleep," she says to me in a low voice of seduction. She stands and walks to me and wraps her arms around me and kisses my biceps. I grab her waist and kiss her neck. She closes her eyes and exhales. I continue to kiss her neck. It tastes salty from the sweat but sweet because it's her. She opens her eyes and looks deep into mine.

We kiss, softly, exploring each
others mouths, caressing each
other's tongues. I get a little more
aggressive with the kissing and try
to back Alexis to the bed but she
stops me.

Alexis breaks the kiss, then
kisses me on the neck, then pats me
on the chest. "Let me go and take a
shower. You know I like to be clean
for you."

Alexis walks into the bathroom
and turns on the shower. I need to
relax my mind because Summer is
still haunting me. I put on my
boxers and T-shirt and walk out of
the room, down the stairs to the
front door where our suitcases are
sitting perfectly against the side of
the door.

I pick up my suitcase and
check to make sure everything I
need is in the bag. Satisfied, I put
the suitcase back and pick up my
camera bag. My Nikon camera and
all my equipment are in the right
place. I put the bag back. At the
moment, I'm satisfied. But, I know
I'll check again in the morning
before we leave.

I hear my cell phone ring. I
walk to the living room where I have
the phone on it's charger. The caller

ID says Summer Boyd. I nervously answer.

"Hello."

With the sweetest, sexiest voice, she says, "Hey, honey, how are you?"

"Summer, what's up?" I say trying to sound calm, cool and collected.

"You're coming to Natalie's grand opening, right?"

"Yeah, I'll get into town tomorrow.   Are you going to be there?" I already knew the answer.

"Of course. That's my girl. You bringing your model friend?"

I know she's not jealous, is she? "Yeah, I'm bringing her, why?"

Summer's tone changes. "No need for attitude, I just wanted to meet the woman who finally got your heart. I mean she does have your heart right? You are happy?"

"Yeah, she has my heart and yes I'm happy."

"Good." Summer sounds as if she has more to say but doesn't know how to say it.

"So is that all you called for after a year, to see if I'm bringing another woman home?" I'm determined to get to the bottom of her middle of the night call.

"Are you still mad at me after all this time?" She asks as if I don't have a reason to be.

Not wanting to yell or get into an argument I simply say, "I'm over it."

She sighs. "No you're not, honey, and neither am I."

"What are you talking about, Summer?"

"Look, I miss you, I miss us, how we used to be. Before we were lovers, we were friends and I don't know..." She trails off, almost like she's fighting back tears.

I hear the shower turning off upstairs and I don't want Alexis to hear me talking to Summer. "Look, why don't I call you when I get to Oakland? We can meet up and talk."

"Okay, I'll see you then. Bye, honey."

Before I can say anything she hangs up. Can't believe she called me out of the blue like that. Man she sounded so good! Just when thought I was getting her off of my mind, she calls. Is this a sign? Perhaps Summer and I should be together. But what about Alexis? She's a good woman and I love her. But I haven't been through all my

ups and downs with Alexis like I've
been with Summer. Alexis has only
known me through the good times.
Alexis doesn't know my hurts like
Summer. When I met Alexis, my
business was already doing good. I
already had my condo. The only
bad thing is that I was still driving
my old car, an old Corolla. It was
bunt orange with hard plastic
interior and no back seat; a real
beater.

I walk back upstairs and stop
by my bedroom where I see Alexis
applying baby oil to her long legs.
She looks sexy as hell sitting on the
edge of the sink, her ass placed on a
dry towel. She slowly massages the
oil into her still wet skin which
makes her glow. My beautiful model
fiancée. Summer looked this good
fresh out the shower.

Damn, I'm thinking of Summer
again. Here I am with this fine
woman in my bathroom, naked and
wanting me to give her the best of
me and all I'm thinking about is
Summer. I have to find a way to get
Summer off of my mind. There is no
way I can give Alexis what she
wants if another woman is on my
mind. Maybe if I just set up a time
where I can meet Summer this

weekend, I won't worry about it anymore.

I walk to my second bedroom, which I've turned, into an office and storage room for all my equipment. I turn on my desk lamp and sit at my mahogany desk and look at my weekend itinerary. I'm going to meet up with Eric, then go to Natalie's store. Maybe Summer will be at the store and we can talk then. No, Alexis is going to be with me, which would be awkward. If I see her at the store, I can just set up a time to meet with her. No, I have a better idea. At the top of my itinerary I write C S (Call Summer) when home. I'll just call her when I get to the Town. I fold the itinerary and set it to the side.

I look up and see Alexis standing in the doorway still just wearing that smile. Her brown sugar skin shimmering under the hallway light. Her seven-day a week workout regimen has paid off big time. Her breasts sit up perfectly without a bra on. Her brown nipples stand at attention. She has her hands on her hips but I'm looking at her perfectly shaved kitty, which makes me smile like a kid in a candy store.

"You were supposed to be waiting in the bed for me," she says as she walks over to the desk.

"Well, you know you take hour long showers sometimes. I figured I had some time to check my schedule."

"Damn it Sean, when are you going to stop being so anal about everything?"

"When I don't have to be."

Alexis leans in front of me, her breast in my face. She turns off the desk lamp. It's dark in the room except for the light coming from the hallway. Alexis kisses me on the lips, then neck, then my ear.

"You know we have to be up and out of here in just a few hours, Alexis. You sure you want to do this?" I'm hoping she says yes but in the back of my mind I know I'm going to be exhausted if we get into it right now. It's already ten and I'm trying to leave by three in the morning so I can get around traffic.

"Shut up Sean. You know you want this just as much as me."

Alexis slides the keyboard and mouse to the side and sits on the desk. I roll my chair a little closer to the desk and softly kiss her lips. Sliding my tongue in I find her pearl and begin the suction, softly, slowly, then faster and harder. She moans, softly at first. She puts one hand on my head and with the other begins to rub her nipple. She likes this more than anything and she should because I'm an expert at it. Her soft moans become louder and louder. She lets me know she's reaching her climax. The moans become words, words become cursing, and cursing becomes heavy breathing until she screams as her body shakes and shivers. I continue the suction until she begs me to stop because of the sensitivity.

I look into her eyes as she smiles. She kisses me as we both taste her sweetness. I stand and pull down my underwear. She drops to the floor and takes me in like a missile pop. I grab her hair and make her stand. I want to be inside of her. I pick her up and sit her back on the desk. She takes me in her hand and slowly eases all of me into her sacred place. I begin to slowly move inside her walls but she looks as if she's not enjoying it as much.

"This is getting uncomfortable," she whispers to me.

"What do you want me to do, Sexy?"

"Take me to the bedroom."

I pull out as she puts her arms around my neck. I wrap an arm around her waist and pick her up. She wraps her legs around my waist as I carry her out of the office and down the hall to my bedroom all while we kiss. We enter the bedroom and I lay her down on the bed.

"Do you want me to get a condom?" I ask, not really caring if she said yes or no.

"No baby, just give it to me."

I think back to the scare we had six months ago. She can sense my uneasiness.

"We're engaged now, you're my husband. Now shut up and give it to me."

Telling me to shut up turned me on and made me want to get a little more aggressive. Before I reenter paradise I lift her legs in the air and over her head. My shoulders keep her from being able to put her legs down or move. I begin to stroke longer and harder as she calls on God for help. When God doesn't intervene, she begins to let a out a curse here and there until her body shakes like an earthquake and she lets out a loud, long yes. Her legs shake and her eyes roll to the back of her head.

After a few moments she catches her breath. "Okay, baby, you're the man. I had enough," Alexis says between heavy breaths and fanning herself.

"I'm not done yet," I tell her as the sweat from our bodies make a large wet stain on top of the comforter.

"I'll finish you off, baby," Alexis says as I let her legs down.

We switch positions and I lay on my back. Alexis climbs on top of me and eases me inside of her walls. She moves slowly at first, trying to find the right rhythm. I put my hands on her ass. She takes my hands away and interlocks them with hers and she lays them on the bed next to my head. She begins to move faster and faster making it hard for me to hold on. She sits up tall and places a hand on my chest and she begins to do what I like best. I know it's about to happen so I warn her which makes her go faster and harder. Before I know it, every muscle in my body tenses up as I explode inside of her. She doesn't stop moving until my muscles relax. She kisses me, then lays on top of me.

Breathing heavy, I wrap my arms around her. "I love you Alexis."

"I love you too, Baby."

As we lay in the bed, naked to the world, I think back to six months ago. It was the first time I had run out of condoms since Alexis and I had started sleeping together the year before. We both really wanted it but our rule was no condom, no love until we're married. But we couldn't help ourselves. I was giving her a bath because she was extremely sore from a two-hour dance show with her students. Before I knew it, we were in the tub together kissing hot and heavy. She got on top of me and began doing what she's great at, moving her hips. Not thinking, I let go inside of her. For the next three weeks we were worried that she might have gotten pregnant, but we dodged a bullet.

Barely moving Alexis and I slide under the covers still holding on to each other. My mind begins to wander back to Summer. I learned a lot about sex with Summer. We tried everything together, even hurting each other on a few occasions because we didn't know what we were doing. Sex with Summer was comfortable, familiar and always adventurous. Now Alexis isn't as adventurous. But I can honestly say she is an expert at pleasing me and giving it to me the way I like it and need it. Now I'm thinking I did, indeed, make the right decision in asking Alexis to marry me. But if it's the right decision, why am I still thinking about Summer?

Chapter 4

Summer Boyd

I sit on my couch looking at a photo of me and Sean. He took it a few months before he moved to LA. We were so happy. My five-foot five body stands in front of his six-foot one and half inch frame. His strong, masculine arms are wrapped around my waist. I remember the way he smelled that day. I had just bought him a bottle of Sean Jean cologne. I also bought him the outfit he's wearing in the picture; a charcoal Sean Jean suit with a light blue Sean Jean dress shirt. It was his birthday, and I needed my man to look good for his birthday.

I smile at the two of us posing for the picture; looking like we were the perfect couple. I let out a sigh. Pictures. Pictures bring back memories and memories bring back old feelings. Feelings of love and being loved. Being with Sean was

the only time I've ever been truly
happy. No man has ever made me
feel the way Sean did, but now
someone else gets to feel what I
used to feel. Man oh man what I
used to feel. Just thinking about it
makes me warm all over. I think
back to all the fun we had growing
up. All the things we shared over
the years. All the sex we had. It
makes me smile with both lips. I
haven't smiled in months. Not since
I found out my ex-boyfriend got
another woman pregnant.

I was actually hoping Jackson
was the one for me. He was smart,
educated, good looking and I
thought all mine. But it turns out
he was messing around with a
couple of different women. I guess I
was foolish to think I was the only
one. Jackson did a lot traveling for
his job as a sports agent. I thought
he was just supposed to get women
for these athletes not sleep with
them himself. Now I'm faced with
starting all over again with someone
else, which scares the hell out of
and irritates me at the same time.

It seems I've always had bad
luck with men. Every man I've
dated turned out to be a cheater, too
controlling, or just not man enough

for me. The one exception was Sean. Sean had always been there for me over the years. He was a good friend and even better lover. Oh, and that first time we had sex on prom night was magical. We must have done it four times that night and then once in the morning. Shoot, I would have done it more but I think I dried the poor boy out. But it was so good, especially by the third time when we got a little rhythm going.

I get chills and goose bumps all over my body. Thinking about sex with Sean makes me horny. It's been over three months since the last time I had sex and my battery operated friend isn't helping, at least not enough. It has been two years, eight months, twenty-one days, and eighteen hours since I felt Sean inside of me. I want him right now but he's hundreds of miles away. But he will be in town tomorrow and I definitely plan to get my groove back. So what if Sean is bringing his little girlfriend. I don't care. I will have Sean in my bed by the end of the weekend.

Sean has always been a little weak when it comes to me. All I ever did was smile at him and he would do whatever, whenever and wherever I wanted. Sean was the perfect buddy. He was loyal, respectful, good-looking, smart and willing to drop another girl in a second if I needed him to. Sean was the guy I could run to for anything. If I needed a few dollars, I would run to Sean. If I needed a ride somewhere, I would run to Sean. If I needed someone to talk to, I could always call Sean. If I needed a shoulder to cry on, I would cry on Sean's. And if I needed to get piped, Sean was my on call plumber.

Maybe, in a sense, I used Sean for my benefit. It wasn't that I didn't love him. I just never felt in love with him, at least not until now. Maybe it's the fact that he seems unattainable now. Maybe it's the fact that I have finally realized that Sean has been the one for me all along and I just didn't know it until now. Maybe it's because I thought Sean would always be there no matter what. So why shouldn't I have a little fun and come back to him later? But now later may be too late.

I drop the picture on the coffee table in front of the couch and walk to the kitchen of my two-bedroom

condo and pour a third glass of
wine. I know I should probably stop
because I know I'm going to wake up
with a horrible hangover if I keep
this up. But the wine seems to give
me a bit of courage. I just got off
the phone with Sean and was ready
to tell him that I was in love with
him when he rushed me off the line.
Probably because of his little model
girlfriend.

"I'll show her. I was around
before you and I'll be around after
you, little miss video tramp."

It's time to pick out the perfect
outfit. One that says come and get
it Daddy. One that will have Sean
staring at me and no one else. I
know I'm supposed to be helping my
girl Natalie get her new store in
order for her grand opening on
Saturday so sweats and a T-shirt
would be appropriate. But with
Sean stopping by, I need something
a little sexier. I think I have the
perfect thing. I pull out a little grey
dress that hugs my thighs and stops
just above the knees. Now I need
something else to set it off. I pull
out a huge black belt and my black
high heel boots. I lay the dress and
belt on the bed and set the heels in
front and admire my selection. Not

bad if I do say so myself. Now if I'm going to wear a sexy dress, I need to feel sexy under the dress. I walk to my dresser and go to my special drawer. I pull out a black satin thong and matching bra. I lay the bra and thong next to the dress and take another sip of my wine.

"Sean is going to want to take me in the back room when he sees this outfit tomorrow."

I'm startled by the sound of my cell phone ringing. I walk into the living room hoping its Sean calling me back. I'm hoping he's calling to tell me how much he's missed me and wants me back. I set my wine down on the glass coffee table and pick up the phone from the cream-colored love seat. I look at the caller ID and lose my excitement. It's not Sean, it's Natalie, my best friend in the world.

"Hey, Nat, what's up?"

"Just calling to make sure you were still coming by tomorrow. You know how you do sometimes."

I know she's not saying I'm a flake. "I'm not going to fake on you, I promise. I'll be there at noon."

Natalie gets loud. "Noon, you trippin. You better have your little self there by nine."

I giggle, proud that I got her. "I'm just playing with you girl. I'll be there."

"You better."

I pause for a second, trying to figure out the best way to ask this question without sounding too excited or worse, desperate. "Do you know if Sean is going to be coming by tomorrow?"

Natalie takes a few seconds to answer. "Look, Summer, I know you're looking to get laid because it's been months since you and Jackson split, but leave Sean alone this weekend."

I roll my eyes even though I know she can't see me. I try to hide my true feelings and try to make it sound like a casual question. "What are you talking about? I just wanted to know if my friend was coming by or not."

Natalie laughs. "You can't even say that over the phone and sound sincere."

"Come on now, Nat, you know how me and Sean do." She should know, I've told her every steamy detail more than once.

"I know and that's why you need to leave him alone. He's happy with his new girl. Let him be for once. This time let it not be about you and what you want. If he is truly your friend like you just said, then let him go."

Alright, now she's annoying me. "Damn, Natalie, you act like I use Sean as my little sex toy."

"You do. The only difference is he doesn't need batteries."

"That's not true, I love Sean and he loves me."

"No, Summer, you love Sean but Sean was in love with you."

"What if I am in love with Sean?"

Natalie pauses for a few seconds. "All I'm asking is that you don't bring any drama this weekend. This is the opening of my very own store and I want it to be drama free. Can you do that for me?"

I hold up my right hand as if Natalie can see it. "I promise. I will not ruin your grand opening. I'll see you tomorrow."

I hang up with Natalie and toss the phone back on the love seat. I grab my glass of wine and take another sip. I walk to my bathroom and begin a bath. While the water runs I go back to the kitchen and refresh my wine glass. I can't believe Natalie would try to stop true love. By her making me promise not go after Sean, she's in turn stopping two people from falling in love. I walk back to the bathroom when my bath is warm and ready for me to get in. I take off my clothes, bra and panties and ease my naked body into the tub.

As I relax in my tub I think about Sean and how he's always been there for me over the years. I think about one of the statements Natalie made. Have I really used Sean for my own personal fun and games? I always thought of Sean as the best type of friend. I could talk him about anything and I could get sex whenever and however I liked. Sean always pleased my mind, soul and body like no one else. No man I have ever been with has been able to do it as good as Sean.

"Natalie doesn't know what she's talking about." I say out loud.

Me and Sean have loved each other for years and I know we are meant to be together. I guess I just never realized how much I loved Sean until now. After so many failed relationships, I have come to the realization that Sean has been the perfect guy for me all along. And he will be mine again. I just have to figure out how to get him away from the model chick. I take another sip of my wine and smile. I've just thought of the perfect idea.

"I'll put it on him one good time and he'll forget all about her."

I know Sean has never been able to resist me when it comes to sex. All I need to do is give him some and he'll be eating out of my hand among other places. I'm not going to let anything stop me, not even the model. I will get Sean back and there's nothing the video vixen is going to be able to do about it but cry. Then after all that, I will finally have what I've always wanted. A stable, reliable man that looks good and sexes me crazy.

Chapter 5

Sean

The drive on I-5 is always long but today it seems even longer. All I can do is think about running into Summer again. I look over to Alexis who is singing along to Michael Jackson's "The Lady in my Life". Her singing is not great but her features are amazing. Even at six in the morning, the glow of her beauty would make the sun jealous. She wears no make up, except for a little strawberry lip-gloss. Her high cheekbones make her smile enjoyable which in turn makes any pain or frustration go away. Her full chocolate brown lips mouth the words of one of MJ's best ballads. She looks at me and smiles as she sings to me, for me, about her.

If Alexis is the lady in my life, what does that make Summer? Summer is, was such a part of me that I can't help but reminisce from

time to time. It's crazy to think out
of all the things Summer and I have
been through we never had a formal
relationship. We filled the void for
each other when we were lonely and
in need of affection. We shared
many first experiences together
because we felt safe and comfortable
with each other. Through it all, we
did love each other. I would do
anything for Summer and I did
everything for her.

I remember the first time we
kissed, it was her idea. She had
been in town for a few weeks and it
was getting close to the end of
summer and the beginning of the
school year. We were about to be in
junior high and I was starting be
more and more interested in girls.
They were all I could think about,
but I had no idea how to approach
them. One day Summer and I were
at the basketball court at the end of
our block, across the street from my
father's church. We were the only
ones on the court. Natalie and Eric
were both out school shopping.

"You ever kissed a girl?"

Summer's question caught me
off guard and I missed my shot. She
grabbed the rebound and dribbled
back to the key. She was, and I

would imagine still, a good basketball player. She beat me several times.

"Yeah, I've kissed a bunch of girls." I lied. Till this day I still don't know why men feel the need to lie about how many girls they can get. In my experience growing up you get shot down more than you actually get the girl. It wasn't until I was in my twenties that I had the confidence that I have now, knowing that if I want her I can get her and if she doesn't want me then it's on to the next one.

"How many?" She asks as she takes the shot and scores.

I toss the ball back to her. "I don't know, too many to count."

"Really." She knew I was lying but wanted to play along. "So if I kissed you right now, you wouldn't be scared?"

She takes another shot and scores but this time I don't grab the ball. I just look at Summer, frozen, unable to move. I couldn't believe this fine girl just said she wanted to kiss me. Okay, she said what if, but in my mind that's the same thing.

Summer walks over and grabs the ball, then walks to me with a smile on her face. "So does that mean you would be scared?"

I wanted to scream hell yeah I'd be scared. But I couldn't; I couldn't say anything. She tosses the ball up and amazingly it goes into the basket and bounces away from us. She moves closer to me, so close I can smell the cherry Kool-Aid on her breath.

"Don't be scared Sean, it would be my first kiss too."

My palms got sweaty, my temperature rose and my nerves became bad and shaky. I can't move but at the same time I feel like fainting. I've thought about kissing Summer since the day she moved to our neighborhood. I even practiced in the mirror a few times. She and Natalie had become best friends and were at my house almost everyday. Summer always stayed a little longer than Natalie and at times she even had dinner with us. She also baby-sat my little sister a few times when my parents were out and I was hanging with Eric. But I never thought that she would want to kiss me.

"What are you waiting for, Sean?" She asks in a soft voice. I couldn't believe she was being so forward about it.

"Are you sure you want to do this?" I ask, hoping she would say no but praying she would say yes.

She smiles at me and gets closer. She presses her lips to mine and holds for what seemed like forever. I don't move, I just let her take the lead. She releases the kiss and smiles at me again.

"See, that wasn't so bad was it?" She says.

Summer walks back and grabs the basketball. I stood in the same place, still frozen. She takes another shot and scores. She smiles again at me, this time my lips spread and I smile the biggest smile ever.

That was our first kiss, just the beginning of many of our firsts. Crazy how things go. I thought I would be the one to initiate my first kiss but I stood there frozen.

"Sean, what are you thinking about?" Alexis asks, which ends my trip down memory lane.

"Nothing." I lie.

"So what are your parents like in person?" Alexis asks. She's only talked with my mother over the phone but she's never been back home with me. This will be their first face-to-face encounter.

I know Alexis and I have been together for two years and it's not like she didn't want to meet my parents, it just was never a good time. I rarely make it back home and when I do it's only for a day or two and I stay in a hotel. With my type of business, I'm usually working seven days a week and with Alexis doing shows or photo shoots, she's usually busy everyday except Sundays.

Alexis has made it a point to go to church every Sunday. I have no problem with Alexis going to church; it's just not for me. The way I see it, God is never there when you need him. He wasn't there to stop my father from making a mistake. He wasn't there to give my mother strength to leave him. Whenever I've needed God's help, He never wanted to help me.

"Are you going to tell me about your family, Sean?" I almost forgot Alexis had asked me a question.

"My mother is cool. I don't understand why she stayed with my dad for so many years." I get a little angry at the thought of what my father did to my mother and our family.

My father was once a popular preacher in the North Oakland community. He was well respected by all of his members. He preached the word with such power and conviction that you could tell God had given him a gift. Then my father, The Good Reverend Winters, went and had an affair with a young woman in the church. He says it was a lapse in judgment, but I believe he just couldn't keep it in his pants.

Tricia Harris was a bombshell. Five-foot six, one hundred twenty pounds and thick in all the right places. She came to the church after leaving a five-year marriage to an abusive husband. She came to my father for counseling and instead of helping her with her problem, The Good Rev took advantage of this young vulnerable woman. He told me it was a one-time thing and it might have been because Tricia disappeared afterwards. My father was able to keep it a secret for about nine months until he got a call telling him that Tricia had just given birth to a baby girl named Andrea. Tricia died in a car accident a few months after Andrea was born. The Good Rev was on the birth certificate as the father. I don't know how he was able to convince my mother, but The Good Rev brought the baby home and has been raising her along with my mother.

This is why I'm not so cool with God. He let The Good Rev, a pastor, give into the temptation of the flesh. Then He didn't give my mother strength to leave. Instead He burdened her with raising my father's child. And God still allows my father to get up in the pulpit and preach the word like he's never done anything wrong. I don't get it and so I decided that I was done being a good Christian boy because it obviously doesn't matter what you do, you're still going to heaven.

"All you ever say about your Pops is that he's a hypocrite." Alexis presses the issue.

I didn't want to talk about my father with her. I get angry when I think about what he put my mother through. It's been eighteen years and my half sister Andrea has grown to be a beautiful woman. I don't blame her for her parent's affair because she didn't make them sleep together. The Good Reverend Winters gave into temptation. He was weak and therefore a failure to my mother, his congregation and me. He's supposed to be our example and above the sins and temptations of the world.

Andrea just graduated from Oakland Technical High School and is trying to figure out whether she wants to go to college or move to LA with me and become a professional dancer. She's been taking dance classes for years and she choreographs all the praise dances at my father's church.

I look over at Alexis who is still waiting for me to tell her about my father and why I don't talk with him. I finally decide I would tell her. If she's going to marry into this family, she might as well know all the dirt.

"My father had an affair."

Alexis' mouth drops. She looks shocked and confused.

I continue. "He slept with a woman who went to our church. The woman got pregnant and got hit and killed by a drunk driver a few months later. My father took the baby in and my mother adopted her about a year later."

Alexis turns her head to the road ahead, her mouth still wide open. I'm wondering now if I should have told her anything. Would she think that was too much information or would she think my family is crazy? Would her new knowledge cause her to break off our engagement less than twenty-four hours after I put the ring on her finger? I'm wondering what's going through her mind. I hope she's not thinking of leaving me, don't know if I could handle that. Then again, it would open a window of opportunity for Summer.

Alexis finally speaks. "Wow! Your parents love must be beyond strong."

"Or my mother is just weak." I don't know why I said that. I don't think my mother is weak. She had to be strong to put up with me as a teenager.

Alexis puts her hand on my thigh. "Your mother has to be a strong woman. Anybody who would take in a child that's not theirs and raise it and care for it makes them a strong person."

"I guess." I had never thought of it that way. My mother could have left my father, but she suffered

the same gossip, stares and
humiliation he did, if not more
because now she's raising his child.

"Do you think you would ever
cheat on me, Sean?"

It was a question I thought she
would have asked a long time ago
but I guess I had earned her trust
and proved that I was for her only.
It also was a question I was afraid to
answer because what if it did
happen one day? Would that make
me a liar?

"No, I wouldn't cheat on you."
This is the best answer. Most
women wouldn't want you to say yes
because that just tells them that
they need to dump you and move on
to the next man. If you answer no,
you keep the peace. The problem is
that most men don't know what they
would do if they were put in that
situation. It's hard to say no when
it's right there for you to take. For
men, sex is like being offered a piece
gum. You're more than likely going
to take it even if you've just gargled
with mouth wash.

"What if you run into
Summer?" Alexis asks

My hand slips on the steering
wheel and the car almost goes into
the other lane. I easily get it back

on track but my mind is racing trying to figure out why Alexis would ask that question. I know of Alexis' insecurities. She had five boyfriends in a row all cheat on her and two of them got other women pregnant while with her. We didn't sleep together for the first six months of our relationship because she truly was trying to be celibate. She had been hurt so many times that she didn't want to jump into bed with just anyone. She had fallen in love with me as I did with her so she wanted to take our relationship to the next level and, of course, I didn't complain. I mean it was hard going six months without sex. Me and the playboy channel became real good friends. But I figured Alexis was the kind of woman worth waiting for. And she has not disappointed me once. She cooks, cleans, gives good love and she gives me space when I need it. She's encouraging, thoughtful, funny and smart. She's all the things Summer was to me, maybe more.

"Summer? What does she have to do with this?"

She rolls her eyes. "Come on, Sean, don't play me for an idiot."

81

She was right to fear the meeting between me and Summer. I don't know what I will do when I see her. I think about our last night together, the love we shared, the love we made. Summer told me she wouldn't be making any more trips to LA because she had met someone new. I don't know why, but that time really hurt me. Our relationship had always been on again off again. We only needed each other when we had no one else. But I was beginning to think maybe Summer and I should try to be together on a full time basis. But it turns out she had other plans. Funny how things work out because a few weeks later I met Alexis.

A few months later, my buddy Eric calls and tells me that Summer had broken up with the guy she left me for. I felt bad for Summer, but by that time Alexis and I had begun seeing each other on a regular basis. I had even broken it off with all of my other lady friends. Soon after, Summer called to say that she would be in LA for a couple of days and wanted to know if she could stay with me. At this point Alexis had a key to my place and was staying over at least three nights a week. I told Summer I couldn't do it. She said she understood but sounded heart broken. Before she hung up she told me when I break it off with Alexis I should give her a call and she'd come visit. Needless to say, that call was never placed.

"What makes you think I want to hook up with Summer?" I want to know if she trusts me or does she really think that I would sleep with Summer when I see her.

"Well you told me you two were just friends with benefits, but you guys never officially ended your relationship."

"We are still friends." I really believe that Summer and I were and are life long friends.

"Oh, really you're friends? So, when's the last time you talked to her?"

I had to think for a second. I didn't want to tell her that Summer called last night while she was in the shower. That would just open an unnecessary can of worms. "It's been almost two years."

"You talked to Natalie yesterday, Eric three days ago. Why has it been two years since you've talked to Summer?"

I just shrug my shoulders. I really couldn't answer that. I mean Summer and I used to talk to each other about everything but after she left the last time, our relationship changed. For the first time we were both in serious relationships, not the casual relationships we had been used to. I admit I was a bit jealous of her newfound love and it made me want to try to find true love myself, and that's why I got serious with Alexis. I guess I hadn't called Summer in the past two years because I was afraid if I did I wouldn't be able to fight the temptation to have her come for a visit.

Alexis looks out the passenger side window. "You still love her, don't you?"

I don't want to lie to Alexis or to myself. That is a hard question to answer. Summer and I always told each other that we loved one another but I told the same thing to Natalie and she said it to Eric on several occasions. We were four friends who grew up on the same street. We were with each other through the good times and the bad times and we stayed friends, so, of course we loved each other. But I think Alexis' question is more of an in love question rather than the love you have for a fellow friend or family member. That I'm not sure of. I just know Summer is still in my thoughts.

"I don't know." It was the best and most honest answer I could give.

Alexis turns and looks at me. I can see her out of the corner of my eye. She's burning a hole in the side of my face with her glare stare. I'm not sure if she wants to hit me, curse me out, yell, or call off the engagement.

"You don't know, Sean Winters? You asked me to marry you and you don't know if you're in love with your ex? What the hell, dude?"

Alexis normally doesn't get angry. She's very good at getting her point across without yelling and screaming. It's one of the things that I love about her. Whenever we disagree on something, we have discussions and not shouting matches. But at this moment, Alexis is mad and her voice is elevated.

"I don't know, Alexis. I don't know if we ever were in love or not."

"Well you better figure it out before we go any further with this engagement."

"What's that supposed to mean?" I ask her.

"I mean you need to confront your feelings. You need to talk to Summer and find out where the two of you stand. I would much rather you find out now rather than marrying me and then regretting never finding out. I love you enough to let you go if you and Summer are meant to be."

I couldn't believe she was saying this. She's telling me to go after Summer and find out if the two of us should be together. Out of respect for Alexis, I was planning to try and keep it casual with Summer when I see her. But if Alexis is giving me free range to explore with Summer, this would mean I wouldn't have to try and sneak a meeting with her during my trip. I could just talk with her and Alexis wouldn't mind. Or is this just a trick to see what I'll say or do? I have to make sure.

"So, you're telling me that you want me to go after Summer?"

"I'm telling you to get her out of your system. But, if you can't, let me know and I'll leave."

I'm still shocked. The woman I am engaged to is telling me she wouldn't even fight for me? Damn, I would fight for her if there was another man in her life she still had feelings for.

"So what if you meet another man and you want to be with him? Are you just going to leave me and expect me to just let you go without a fight?"

She puts her hand up and shows off her engagement ring.

"I am wearing your ring, Sean, which means there is no other man out there for me. But I guess you don't feel the same because Summer may be for you."

She got me with that one. She didn't have anyone else holding a piece of her heart. It was all me. But, me, I didn't know if I still had someone else in my heart. Summer was the only woman I had been with consistently through out high school and college. Summer and I learned about our bodies together. We learned how to please each other. I know that I am in love with Alexis but I just can't stop thinking about the love I had with Summer.

We drive in silence for a while. Alexis stares at her ring, probably wondering if she is going to have to take it off or will it be there for the rest of her life. I feel bad because I can't just fix this with an "I'm sorry" or an "I love you." Alexis needs to know that my heart is fully and completely hers, but I can't tell her it is. Summer has been such a major part of my life for twelve years. I can't just write her off. Maybe Alexis is right. Maybe I do need to confront Summer and discuss where we stand. But how do I get her out of my system? A hug, a kiss, a sexual encounter? I don't know, but something has to be done and quickly because I need to know if Alexis is truly the woman I am supposed to marry.

I try to break the silence by changing the subject. "Did you call and confirm our hotel reservations?"

Alexis turns and looks out the passenger side window. I couldn't tell if she was mad or avoiding the question.

"Alexis, did you hear me?"

Alexis turns back to me and reluctantly tells me that she

canceled our hotel reservations. I nearly hit the roof. Where did she expect us to stay?

"I talked with your mom yesterday and she said we can stay with them."

"Alexis, why would you do that? You know that me and my father don't get along." At this point I have gone from angry to furious. When was she planning on telling me we didn't have a hotel to stay in? And who gave her permission, yes I said permission, to talk to my mother and make arrangements for us?

"I know you and your father don't get along. That's why I wanted us to stay with them. You need to patch things up with your father because you never know when the good Lord would decide to take him away and you can't patch things up."

"Don't give me the good Lord stuff right now, Alexis. You have no right to get into my family business."

Alexis puts her ring finger in my face again. "When you put this on my finger you gave me the right to get into all of your business including family business."

Alexis further went on to explain how she wanted me to forgive my father and move on from the hurt and pain. She told me what it was like for her to grow up without a father and having a mother who was never around. She was left with an older sister and younger brother to fend for themselves because their mother worked two jobs. She told me she dreamed of having a close family because her family was not. Her mother died at fifty-five from a heart attack. Her big sister moved to Atlanta with her boyfriend, and her little brother is in prison for selling drugs. All of these things happened before she was twenty years old. She decided to move from Chicago to LA to become a dancer and wound up becoming a dancer, teacher, choreographer and a print model.

"You don't realize how important family is until they're not around." She finishes, while wiping tears from her eyes.

I realized how important it was to Alexis for me to try and mend my relationship with my father. I agreed to go along with staying with my parents for her but I doubt my father and I will be able to resolve all of our issues in one weekend.

I don't know if I like the fact that Alexis took it upon herself to set this whole thing up. I only planned on making a quick appearance at the church anniversary ceremony on Sunday. I didn't think I would be spending the entire weekend with my parents. My mother, I didn't mind so much. But my father was the last person I wanted to spend any time with. I thought these three days would be fun. I'd introduce Alexis to my friends and my mother. Then Alexis would spend the rest of the time traveling through my old stomping grounds. Now I'm having second thoughts about this weekend because not only do I have to deal with my parents, I need to talk to Summer about where we stand. I hope I am able to survive it all.

Chapter 6

Sean

I park the car on the street in front of my parents house. It looks exactly the same. A two story white house with red trim on the windows and roof and red cement steps that lead to the front and back doors. I sit and stare at the house for a few moments, unable to move. I hadn't really spoken with my father since I moved to LA five yeas ago. Alexis leans over and kisses me on the cheek and turns off the engine.

"It will be okay, baby." She tries to reassure me but I knew better. She doesn't know my father like I know him. He walks around pointing out everyone else's problems but never talks about his affair. The Good Reverend Winters acts as if he does no wrong and everyone else is doing bad.

I take a deep breath and look at Alexis. I lean in and kiss her on the lips. The taste of her strawberry lip-gloss makes me a little upset. I am now realizing that because we are staying with my parents we will probably not make love the entire weekend. The walls are paper-thin and my old bed squeaks too much for us to get away with anything freaky for the next three days. That just makes me want to see Summer even more. I mean at least she has her own place so if we wanted to get down, we'd have privacy.

"You ready?" I ask her but I am really asking to myself.

She smiles at me. "Let's go."

I pop the trunk and the two of us get out of the car. I look down 44th Street and it looks quiet, too quiet for a Friday in August. There are several cars on the street but I see no children playing. No kids riding bikes or playing football in the street. I remember when I was kid, there were always kids running around. Now I guess all the kids have grown up and moved on and there are no new kids to take their place. It kind of makes me sad because 44th and Market used to be a lively street and now it's as quiet as a cemetery.

I close the car door and grab our suitcases from the trunk. Alexis has one of those suitcases with the wheels and I made use of them because her bag is extremely heavy for a three-day stay. We walk up the driveway, past The Good Reverend Winters and my mother's car. We walk up the red steps to the front door. I ring the bell, but like during most of my childhood, the bell wasn't working so I had to bang on the screen door.

I could hear my mother calling from inside. "Just a minute."

My mother's voice was welcoming and inviting. I felt a little calmer when I heard her. Maybe I'd spend more time with her this weekend and less with my father. Hopefully he would be too busy with his church anniversary to spend much time at home. Wishful thinking. Knowing my father, he was ready to meet Alexis and grill her on her choice of careers, especially her modeling half-naked at times. Not that she should be ashamed, she has a beautiful body and I know every part of it.

A few seconds past before I heard my mother unlock the three locks on the main door. The main door opens and my mother then unlocks the two locks on the screen door and opens it. I wonder why my parents still lived in this neighborhood after so many years. When you have to put five locks on your doors and have an alarm system, something is not right with where you live. My father says it's his home, he owns it and he will die in it. I say he's crazy because he and my mother could afford to live in a nicer neighborhood where they wouldn't need three different keys to get in the house.

"My baby!" My mother shouts with glee. She opens her arms and gives me a big hug and kiss on the cheek. I look at my mother and see the years have been good to her. She is in her mid-fifties but looks as if she could be in her late thirties. She was always a health nut and was in the gym at least three days a week. She looks toned but not muscular, and I'm glad because huge muscles are not a good look on women. Her short black hair looks wet as if she just got out of the shower. She probably just got back from the gym.

She is a few inches shorter than Alexis so she has to reach up to hug her. Alexis bends down to meet her halfway. "How are you Mrs. Winters? It's so good to finally meet you in person."

My mother ushers us into the house. "Oh, Alexis, child you call me Toni." Toni is short for Antoinette. She's always gone by Toni. I think I was around ten the first time I heard someone call her Antoinette. One of those bill collectors calling on the phone one Saturday morning. I guess I lied and didn't know it when I told him that there was no Antoinette here and he had the wrong number.

"Okay, Toni." Alexis says with a smile while holding my mother's hand.

We are now standing in the kitchen, which is the first room you enter when walking into the Winters' home. My mother must have recently upgraded the kitchen with all new black appliances including a new dishwasher. The beige cabinets and drawers match perfectly with the black table and beige chairs. They have also put in fake hardwood floor the same color as the cabinets. I think to myself this looks good but why did they decide to change when I left? I had to deal with white

cabinets that looked grey because of
dirt. We had an old tan kitchen
table that was always falling apart.
I remember my father every few
months putting another nail or glue
on the table or one of the chairs.
And the linoleum floor had several
holes from wear and tear. I can also
remember being the dishwasher.
That's why when I moved out, one of
the main things I wanted in my own
place was a dishwasher.

"Mom, you really have this
place looking nice! When did you do
all of this?"

"After you moved out. If you
didn't insist on staying in a hotel
every time you came to visit, you
would have seen it," my mother tells
me with a hurt in her voice. I know
she didn't like the void between my
father and me. She could never
understand why I couldn't forgive
The Good Reverend Winters if she
could. I guess I just wasn't ready to
forgive.

"Well, that's all going to
change, Toni." Alexis begins.
"There will be no more avoiding
family time as long as I'm around."

My mother looks Alexis over
and smiles. I can see she already
approves. Her thumb hits Alexis

ring finger. She releases Alexis
hand and looks down. I can't tell
whether she's happy or sad. I think
she's just in shock.

"And I see you're going to be
around for a while," my mother
says. "When did my son put that
ring on your finger because he sure
didn't tell me you two were
engaged?"

Alexis looks down at her finger
and smiles at me. "I guess I forgot
to take it off. We wanted it to be a
surprise."

She forgot to take it off, yeah
right. I know women well enough to
know that once that ring is on their
finger, it's not coming off unless
they need to get it re-sized because
of weight gain or weight loss.

I jumped in. "I wanted to make
it a surprise, but Ms. Nosey here
found the ring last night so I had no
choice but to propose."

"Well, welcome to the family,
Alexis." My mother hugs Alexis,
then me. She is beyond happy. My
mother has been hinting at me
marrying Alexis for the past year.
Even though she had never met her
in person, she would tell me that
Alexis must be marriage material
because she's the longest

relationship I've had. Which, to my mother, is true because she only knew Summer and I dated in high school for a few months. After high school, Summer and I became friends with benefits and my mother need not ever know that.

I walk down the long hallway to the first room, my old bedroom, to put the bags down. I am surprised to see that my room has been turned into an office with a desk, bookshelf, computer, a couch and a couple of chairs.

"I guess you're wondering where you are going to be sleeping?" My mother says while still standing in the kitchen. I guess she wanted me to be surprised to find that nothing was the same in the house since I left.

I walk back to my mother with bags in hand. "What happened to my room?" I ask. I am a little upset. I don't really know why I'm angry. I don't live here anymore. I guess I just thought they would miss me so much that they would keep my room the same for the memories. Now I can't remember what my room looked like before.

My mother explained that The Good Reverend Winters turned my bedroom into his study a year after I moved out. She said he never had a home office and would do most of his work at the church. Even though his church was right down the street, he was tired of having to get up, get dressed and go down to the church. So when I decided to start staying in hotels when I came to visit, The Good Reverend Winters decided on a new use for my room. My mother went on to say they got rid of my old bed and anything that seemed of no value to me, like my boom box, DVD player and television. They took my school year books and awards and put them in a box in the garage.

"So, we don't have any place to sleep?" I asked still a little upset and hurt that my parents destroyed my room without asking. I know they didn't need my permission, but what if I wanted to come and get some of my old things before they threw them away?

"Oh boy, please, I wouldn't leave my baby out like that." My mother walks us over to a door next to the kitchen, which leads downstairs. My parents had renovated the downstairs to be a small apartment. My mother always opened her doors to those going through tough times. She is a social worker and first lady of my father's church so she was always running into people down on their luck. As of late though, no one had rented the downstairs area.

My mother unlocks the door and leads us down the stairs to the small living area. It has everything you would need to get on your feet. There is a small refrigerator and freezer, a little hot plate, cabinets to store food, a card table with four metal chairs around it, a small TV, a sofa bed and small closet with a three-drawer dresser. There is also a small bathroom with only enough room for a sink, toilet and a tiny shower.

"You're going to make us stay down here?" I ask a little in shock. The place wasn't bad for someone down on their luck but I have been spoiled with my new life in LA. My photography business has bought me a comfortable lifestyle. I don't know if I can handle sleeping on a sofa bed.

"This is fine, Toni." Alexis can see the disappointment on my face but she was trying to make the best of it. One thing about Alexis is that she never got spoiled. Even though we are both able to get the things we want and need, she held on to the times when she didn't have anything and couldn't get it even if she wanted it. This isn't bad to her and it shouldn't be bad to me considering I was living here five years ago. My parents have just recently begun to have a little extra money. I grew up poor, but I never wanted to live that way again. So, to me, this is a step back.

"Well, you kids get unpacked. I'm sure you want to get out and see your friends. Eric has already called three times this morning to see if you've arrived." My mother says as she begins to walk towards the stairs.

"Hey, Mom, where's The Good Reverend Winters?" I asked, because I hadn't seen him or Andrea, but his car was in the driveway. I guess I was thinking he might be in his bedroom avoiding me.

"He took Andrea to get the brakes on her car fixed and to get an oil change." My mother went back up stairs and closed the door behind her.

I set the bags on the sofa bed and began to unpack. I thought back to when I graduated high school and was headed to college. The Good Reverend took me to get my brakes fixed, the oil changed and a tune up all in the same week. I wonder if he was giving Andrea the same speech he gave me about being responsible. He didn't want me to be dependent on him for everything, especially since I decided to live in the dorms my freshman year at San Francisco State University.

"Are you mad at me?" Alexis breaks my train of thought.

"Lets see, we went from staying at the beautiful Marriot Hotel to staying in a transit home."

She throws one of her socks at me. "Don't be a jerk. And stop acting like you're better than this. You grew up in this house."

"Yeah, but not down here." I remind her.

"Let's just make the best of it, okay." Alexis walks over to me and wraps her arms around my neck. She gives me a quick peck on the cheek. She knows I'm still upset so she's trying calm me down with her touch.

"I just didn't want to stay here."
Her touch always works. I'm
calming down and things don't look
so bad at the moment.

She kisses me softly on my lips.
"It shouldn't matter where we stay
as long as we are together."

Yeah, but we can't be together
in this place. Alexis can be a bit of a
screamer during sex and even if we
started to get into something, I'd be
worried someone would come down
stairs unannounced. This is going
to be a long weekend if I can't have
sex. I'm no sex fiend but I was at
least hoping to get something this
weekend, especially since we are
now engaged.

I hear a car pull into the
driveway. I gently break away from
Alexis and walk to a small window
next to the separate entrance to the
apartment to see my sister and
father getting out of a fifteen year
old Honda Civic. I begin to go for
the door that leads into the driveway
to greet them but change my mind.
I turn back to Alexis who has gone
back to unpacking our bags. I feel
nervous about Alexis meeting my
father now. What would he think
about her modeling and the videos
she's done? All of her work has

been, in my view, tasteful, but she has been filmed and photographed in just lingerie on several occasions.

"Was that your father?" Alexis asks.

I reluctantly nod my head.

"Well, are we going to go up to meet him?" She has so much excitement in her voice it's almost annoying. It's not like she's meeting the President or anything. She's just meeting my hypocrite father, The Good Reverend Winters.

"I thought you wanted to unpack." I try to stall the inevitable. I know it's impossible. I can already hear my mother talking to my father and my sister about Alexis.

"I'm pretty much done, Sean. We only brought a few things. It's not like we're moving in. We're just here for three days."

She had a point and it looked as if she had everything out except for our bathroom essentials: toothbrush, toothpaste, mouthwash, floss, hair grease and hairbrush.

"Okay, but don't say I didn't try and warn you about The Good Reverend Winters."

Alexis sucks her teeth and smiles at me. She walks over to me and takes my hand in hers. She begins to move quickly forcing me to pick up speed. We walk up the stairs and open the door that leads to the main house. We walk in and see my parents sitting at the kitchen table and my sister Andrea standing behind my mother's chair.

Everyone stops talking and stares at us for a moment. Andrea smiles and quickly walks over to me and hugs me causing Alexis to release my hand. Andrea stands about five-eight, making her about two inches shorter than Alexis. Andrea also has a dancer's body, real thin but toned. She probably works out with my mother.

"Hey, Sean, how's my big bro?" Andrea was up to something. I usually don't get a big hug and a "How are you doing" from her. Normally when I come to visit it's a quick hug and a "I'm going to the mall, see you later." Andrea either wanted something from me or at eighteen she was finally maturing.

"What's going on Drea? This is my fiancée Alexis."

Alexis extends her hand only to be met with a huge hug from Andrea. "I know, mom was just telling us that you were engaged."

I don't know why but it still sounds strange to hear Andrea call my mother mom when she knows that's not her biological mother. I guess since Andrea's mom died when she just an infant and my mother adopted her when she was a year old, my mother is the only mother she's ever known or will know. But I would have thought my mother would have demanded that Andrea not call her mom. When my parents told Andrea the whole story when she was twelve years old, Andrea just said my mother was the only mother she will ever know and to her that was fine. But, for me, it's still difficult to hear.

"It just happened last night." Alexis tells her with a giant smile. She has gotten even happier after the hug from Andrea.

My father stands. He's my height but a little wider. Stress over the past eighteen years has made him age at least thirty years. He has a full head of grey hair with a matching beard. He walks with a cane due to a car accident seven years ago that almost claimed his life. You would think after almost losing my father I would find a way to forgive him for his affair but I still can't bring myself to do so.

He uses his cane to walk to us. He extends his hand to Alexis and they shake. "Nice to meet you. I've heard a lot about you."

"Yes, I'm sorry I was never able to make it up here when Sean would come to visit, but I would be away in a show or in a photo shoot."

"You model underwear don't you?" My father rudely asks.

"Daddy!" Andrea shouts.

"What kind of question is that?" I ask almost ready to fight my old man.

My mother walks over and pops him on the shoulder. "Mind your manners, Ronald."

Alexis puts her hands up to silence our anger. "It's okay everybody. I have done some print ads in lingerie and have been in a few music videos in next to nothing."

"Ya see, I didn't ask her about anything she hasn't done." The Good Reverend Winters was trying to find out what buttons he could push on Alexis but she wasn't having it.

"But you didn't ask her about her dancing or choreography." I say, trying to give Alexis more ammunition to shoot my father's rude comments down. I would love to give her a real gun so she could literary shoot him down.

"You choreograph too?" Andrea asks with extra excitement. She has dreamed of being a professional dancer and choreographer.

"Yes, I do dance and have done choreography on two stage musicals that toured the country."

"Think you can help me with this one move I can't seem to get for the church anniversary this weekend?" Andrea becomes timid, not knowing if she has put her foot in her mouth by asking for help.

The Good Reverend Winters puts his foot in his mouth for her. "She's a Hollywood dancer, she probably doesn't know how to praise dance."

My mother slaps my father on his shoulder even harder this time, almost making him lose his balance. My blood begins to boil. Alexis has only seen me angry a handful of times but she knows my boiling point. Before I can get a word out Alexis steps in.

"Reverend Winters, my love for dancing comes from me being a little girl doing praise dances in church. I can assure you that I can help Andrea with her dance without making it too Hollywood."

I think I just fell in love with Alexis all over again. She just put The Good Reverend Winters in his place in the most polite but stern way possible. My mother looks at Alexis and I can tell she's impressed at her comeback to my father. Andrea looks at Alexis as if she is her hero. My father realizes that he's not going to be able to push any of Alexis' buttons so he just smiles.

"Sean, you better keep this one." He tells me this as if I'm not already engaged to her or that he has any say in who I should be with. And he definitely can't tell me what to do anymore.

"So I take it you approve of me?" Alexis asks with a smile on her face.

The Good Reverend Winters smiles, then slowly walks out of the kitchen, down the hall, towards his bedroom. He walks slowly with his head down, defeated. I feel proud that my fiancée is the first person I've seen make my father speechless. She is going to fit in well with this family.

My mother hugs Alexis. "Welcome to the family girl. We are going to get along great."

I get a text on my phone. I check and it's from Summer. She wants to know if I made it in town yet.

"I'll let you guys talk for a second. I'm going to go to the bathroom real quick." I quickly walk back downstairs, closing the door behind me. When I'm sure no one is following me or can hear me, I call Summer back.

"Hey, you get my text?" Summer says sounding sweeter than honey.

"Yeah, I'm here." I tell her trying to keep my cool. I don't want to sound too excited that we were talking.

We sit silent for a few moments, not really knowing what to say. I want to tell her I want to see her now. I want to take her to a room, rip all her clothes off and give her the business. I want to make her moan. I want to make her scream. I want to make her call out my name in three different languages. At this moment, I want her more than anything in the world.

111

"I'm sorry I called so late last night," she breaks our silence, "That wasn't right and I won't do it again."

"It's cool, don't trip."

"I really want to see you today."

I don't know what to say. I want to see Summer but I'm not sure how I will act when I see her. A piece of me still wants to be with Summer but the other part of me wants to leave our relationship in the past. I want to move on with Alexis but I've never totally moved on from Summer.

"I don't know about today, Baby Girl, I'm showing Alexis around." I can't believe I just slipped up and called Summer by my pet name for her. I hope she didn't notice. But if she did notice, I wonder how she feels about me calling her Baby Girl?

"Well, are you going to be going over to Natalie's store today?"

"Yeah, I was thinking of stopping by Natalie's store." I tell her. I figure if I meet Summer at Natalie's store then I wouldn't be compelled to sex her on sight.

"Okay, well I'll be there this afternoon, we can talk then." Summer sounds so anxious to meet. I wonder what she really wants to

112

tell me in person. It can't be that serious, can it? It's not like she had my baby and never told me, right? If that were the case, Eric or Natalie would have said something. It could be that after two years she's finally ready to admit she made a mistake when she left me to be with another man right after we made love.

"You know Alexis is going to be with me? I don't know if that's a good idea." I tell her. The last thing I need is some crazy drama while I'm up here.

"Don't worry about her. You won't after we talk anyway." Summer has this sexy but sinister tone to her voice. It makes me a little nervous but turns me on at the same time.

"Alright, I'll be there this afternoon." I tell her, giving in to her request to meet, even though my fiancée will be with me. I wonder if I should tell Summer that I'm engaged. Probably not, because it may ruin any chance of finding out what's really on Summer's mind. If she knows I'm engaged she may hide how she feels and just wish me luck. I need to know if she still wants me. I need to find out if I still want her.

"Okay, Honey, I'll see you there." Summer hangs up the phone.

I stand in the little apartment and just think to myself. I wonder if I'm making a mistake in trying to see Summer. I hear Alexis up stairs laughing with my mom and sister. She's such a good person with such a good heart and I may be in route to breaking it. Alexis is a good woman but Summer is my first love, my first everything. Summer was my best friend and Alexis is my best friend. Both women are good for me but I can only allow one of them to have my heart.

I get another text message. This time it's from Eric asking when I will be at his club. I text him back that I'm on my way. I walk to the stairs and reflect for a second. I've been home for about an hour and already I've had a run in with my dad, I've gotten stuck in this makeshift apartment instead of a nice hotel, Eric is blowing up my phone like a scorned ex-lover and my first love wants to see me. "This is going to be a long weekend," I say to myself as I walk up the stairs and into the kitchen. All three ladies are sitting at the kitchen table.

"We should get going. Eric just text me." I tell Alexis.

"Okay." Alexis turns to Andrea. "When we come back, I'll show you some moves that may be able to help."

Andrea gets all excited again. "Thank you."

"Don't thank me. We're about to be sisters. I'm happy to do it." Alexis stands and walks to me.

"Well, you kids get on out of here, dinner will be ready when you get back," my mother says walking us to the front door.

Alexis and I exit the house and get into my car.

"So, you ready to call the wedding off yet?" I ask her.

"What? No way. I love your mother and your sister and I have dancing in common."

"And my father?" I ask. To me, he may be the only reason for Alexis to call of the wedding and head home.

"Your father likes to mess with people but he's harmless."

I lean in and kiss her softly. I guess if she has survived the first meeting with my family and hasn't run away, then maybe she's strong enough to become a part of this

family. I start the car and head
towards Eric's club. I want to make
it a quick meeting with Eric because
I want to make it to Natalie's store.
I have missed and want to see
Natalie but I really need to see
Summer.

Chapter 7

Alexis

Sean decides to take me to do a little sight seeing as we drive towards his friend Eric's club. He makes a left on 40th and Market and drives down past M. L. K. Boulevard, the Bay Area Rapid Transit station or BART and Telegraph Avenue. The streets are a mix of run down houses with brown grass and big beautiful homes with nice lawns. I see what seems to be several homeless sitting on bus benches or just on the sidewalk. We make it to Broadway and a 76 Gas Station. Sean makes a right and we drive past Kaiser Hospital, which seems to take up several blocks. It even looks like they are doing construction across the street. He tells me there was a shopping center called the MB Mall there before the construction started.

We continue down Broadway and pass by several car dealerships. Sean tells me the strip is called

Broadway Auto Row. I try to find
my next car as we pass the
Mercedes Benz dealership. We pass
by the Paramount Theatre which is
a large theatre where Sean says all
of Tyler Perry and David E. Talbert
plays come when they're in town. I
love gospel plays and I hope to be in
one soon. I would have to play a
character that doesn't sing though.
He tells me that there are comedy
shows and concerts almost every
weekend. I tell him we have to go
there one day soon.

We finally make it to Jack
London Square. Sean turns left
onto Second Street and finds a park
on the street.

We walk about a block and half
to a small building called "After
Hours." Sean tells me Eric has
always been the go to guy for
throwing parties and events. He
also tells me that Eric is the only
one of them who opted not to go to
college. He got his business license
and started planning parties. Sean
admits he was extremely jealous of
Eric while he was in college. While
Sean was struggling in school and
trying to save money, Eric was
pulling in thousands a month. By
the time Sean graduated, Eric had

this club, a house, a luxury car and dozens of tailor made suits. Even with all of this, Sean says Eric never changed. He never acted as if he was better than him and he always had him on the VIP list for all his parties.

Sean and I walk into the small club and we're immediately on the dance floor; good thing the club isn't open right now. There is a small stage to the right of us. Sean says Eric lets a lot of local up and comers perform. To the right of us are several tables and chairs. Straight ahead is a large bar. Sean spots Eric sitting on a bar stool looking over some papers. He's wearing a nice navy blue suit, a black button up shirt with no tie and a pair of Prada shades. He sees us and waves us over. I take Sean's hand as he leads me to the bar.

"What's up, Family?" Eric says as he stands and greets Sean with a handshake and hug.

"Hey, Eric. I want you to meet Alexis." He brings me a little closer.

"Hello, Eric." I say with a smile and extended hand.

"Well it's about time." Eric gives me a hug. "If Sean told me you were on tour again I was going to think he was making you up."

"I'm totally real. Good to finally meet you. Sean is always talking about you."

Eric looks Sean up and down then back to me. "Well it must be good things because you didn't slap me."

We all share in a laugh. I look around again. I notice a VIP section off to the right of the bar behind closed doors. It also must be the way to Eric's office.

Sean did tell me all about Eric, the good and the bad. He says Eric has always been a true and loyal friend and has always had his back. He goes on to say Eric is also a pretty boy which got him into a lot of trouble with women. He told me he can't count all the times he had to cover for Eric because he was seeing three and four women at once. He's had baseball bats swung in his direction, almost run over by cars and even shot at a couple of times all because he was with Eric when one of his girls confronted him about cheating. Sean used to think Eric just had bad luck but then realized Eric brought all of that drama on himself. All that changed when he met Krystal.

"So, where's Krystal?" Sean asks.

Krystal is Eric's longtime girlfriend. They have been together at least five years without Eric even mentioning marriage as far as Sean knows. It seems that Krystal has made Eric give up a lot of his player ways. Sean told me Krystal is college educated, strong, independent and a manager of a bank. She and Eric have been living together for the past three years and Krystal is now seven months pregnant with their first child.

"She's over at Natalie's store helping her set up," Eric tells Sean as he goes back to looking at his papers.

"So, what was so urgent that you needed me to come down here when I got to the Town?" Sean asks.

"Man, I wanted you to bring Alexis by is all. You've been keeping her under wraps, Family." Eric says, not looking up from his paperwork.

I see Sean get annoyed. I think it's cute. All of Sean's friends want to check me out to make sure he's making the right choice being with me. I didn't have that until Simone and I became close. Perhaps if I did, I wouldn't have made so many mistakes when it came to men. Sean, however, doesn't think it's cute and cops an attitude with his friend.

"You made me drive to downtown Oakland so you can meet my woman?"

"I'm flattered." I say as I grab Sean's hand. I want to make sure Sean doesn't get too upset. It's not that big of deal to me. I also don't see why Sean got upset to begin with. The only other place we have to go is to Natalie's store. It's barely afternoon so we have plenty of time to stop by and see his other friend. But then it pops in my head. Summer is more than likely going to be there and Sean wants to see her.

Eric signs the bottom page of his paperwork and stands. He's a few inches taller than Sean but about thirty pounds lighter. They are about the same complexion and both go for the clean-shaven look, though it looks like Eric is in need of a shave right now.

"What did you expect? You've been dating this woman for two years and this is the first time I'm meeting her. You met Krystal on our first date."

"That's only because you double dated with me and Summer." Sean looks as if he just put his foot in his mouth.

There is a long period of silence because Sean and Eric both feel a little awkward. I have felt Sean trying hard not to mention Summer since we had the little tiff in the car on the way to Oakland. Eric, on the other hand, looks like he's not sure if Sean has ever mentioned Summer to me.

I finally break the obvious tension in the room. "Don't worry, Eric, I know all about Summer."

Eric looks at me in awe. "And you're not a little jealous or irritated she's going to be up here this weekend?"

Sean punches Eric in the arm. "Man what's wrong with you?"

"What?" Eric asks as he rubs his arm.

"You're always putting your foot in your mouth. Like that time you called that girl in school 'Lazy Boobs' because one was higher than the other," Sean says.

Even though that sounds mean, it made me laugh a little.

"I'm just saying, if I were at an event and one of Krystal's ex-boyfriends was there, then there might be a fight at said event."

"Why?" I ask. "If Krystal is with you, then she's with you, just like Sean is with me. I'm not going to fight someone over what is already mine."

I say that but I'm a little worried about Summer. I don't want to have to fight over Sean, but if Summer tries anything I may have to put hands on her and not in a Godly way. But I shouldn't be worried because Sean is with me and has put a ring on my finger.

Eric tries to counter my last remark. "What if it was that person's before and they want it back?"

"Alright, Eric, that's enough." Sean tells him.

"No, I'll answer." Alexis says. "In that case, it is up to the person I'm with whether they want to go backwards with their ex or move forward with me. And I believe that we all naturally walk forward."

Eric begins to bow to me. I laugh and make Eric stand. He stands and looks at Sean.

"I like her. Hold on to her." He tells Sean.

"I plan to. We're getting married." Sean tells him pointing towards my ring which I hold up for Eric to see.

Eric pulls his shades down and just stares at the ring for a second. Sean shakes him to try and get some type of response out of him. He turns and looks at me but doesn't say a word. I slowly put my hand down, my smile turning into a frown.

"Eric, say something man." Sean says.

Eric blinks then calmly says, "I need a drink."

Eric pushes his shades back over his eyes and walks behind the bar and begins to pour himself a drink. He offers us one but we both decline. Sean and I both sit on bar stools.

"What's wrong, E?" Sean asks.

"First Natalie goes and gets married, now you. What's next? Summer going to get hitched?"

Sean asks, "What about you and Krystal? It seems only right

that after five years and a baby that you would be thinking of marrying Krystal."

"Me and Krystal? Married? That's a big step." He says as he finishes off his drink.

"And living together and having a child isn't a big step?" I ask him. To me it just seems like he's doing it backwards. "You're afraid of marriage aren't you?" I ask after Eric doesn't respond.

"Now why would I be afraid?" Eric asks pouring himself another drink.

Sean has told me Eric comes from a broken home. His father never married his mother, and never really lived with them unless he didn't have anywhere else to go. He was what the Temptations called a rolling stone. He was a musician and traveled all over the country. Eric knows of four brothers and three sisters his dad fathered. He's met two living here in the Bay Area. After a while, Eric's mother moved on with another man who treated Eric as if he were his own. But he never married Eric mother either. Sean told me he thinks this is why Eric can't commit to marriage. His biological father and the man who helped raise him never married his mother.

"I don't know why you would be scared but I can tell you are." I continued to try and make Eric face his fear.

"To me, marriage is nothing but false hope for the people involved."

I smile. "Please explain."

"The woman has hope that the man will be faithful and it's rarely the case because every man will eventually cheat. The man has false hope that his woman will always be a freak in the bed. But they do all of that freaky stuff to get you, but after the wedding all that freaky stuff becomes nasty and they don't do those kinds of things. Which in turn causes the man to go and find someone else who will be his freak."

I wondered if that's why Sean's father had an affair. Was he not being satisfied at home? I don't think I will be like that. I love pleasing Sean too much to think it's nasty. And the way Sean goes down on me, I pray, will never stop. I wouldn't call myself a freak but I like to do whatever necessary to make sure Sean is satisfied. The only things I'm totally against are threesomes and doing it in a public place. Sean has brought that up but I quickly dismissed those fantasies. With the exception of those two, Sean has told me I've fulfilled all his fantasies. I guess the public place got fulfilled in a way because we did it on a plane before.

"Did you ever think that a woman wants her man to be more romantic or more exciting in bed? Maybe the man is doing the same old thing in bed and she wants something new or she doesn't want it at all."

"Now, Alexis, that's false hope. A man doesn't change because he gets married. If he's doing the same moves before marriage, then he's going to do the same moves after marriage." Eric smiles and walks to the other side of the bar to us.

I respond by saying, "In that case, the woman needs to communicate with her man and tell him what she wants."

Eric laughs, "Communication, that's the other problem. Neither the man or woman communicates what they want so they both walk around frustrated because they feel the other person should be able to know what they want. Contrary to popular belief, men and especially women are not mind readers."

I stand. "So what you're saying is that men and women need to communicate more?"

Eric nods. "Exactly. Stop being scared to say what's on your mind."

I walk to Eric and put my hands on his shoulders. "So have you communicated to Krystal that you're afraid to get married?"

Eric looks over to Sean and sarcastically says, "I don't like her anymore."

I take that as a compliment.

Chapter 8

Sean

After leaving Eric's lounge, Alexis and I walk around Jack London Square for a few minutes. We walk past Kincaid's Restaurant and I start to think about all the times Summer and I went there to eat. It made me think about how far we had come, because you can't go to Kincaid's without spending a hundred dollars or more. Summer and I started to go to Kincaid's when we had a little money. It made me think back to our first date, before we could afford Kincaid's.

I was sixteen, had my first car and a license to drive it. It was the summer before my junior year of high school and I felt grown. All I did was run errands for my mother and drive to the movie theatre in Emeryville or to the Jack n the Box on Telegraph Ave, but I felt like an adult because I was driving.

I remember standing in the driveway of our home washing my black 1989 Honda Accord. I saw Summer across the street sitting on her porch. I couldn't tell if she was watching me or if she was daydreaming. All of a sudden she got up and walked over to me.

"You want to take me out to eat?"

I couldn't tell if it was a question or a demand. Either way I was willing. We had moved on from the first kiss four years prior to feeling each other up a few times a week. We still weren't a couple, just a couple of kids experimenting with our bodies, which had both changed in four years.

I had gotten a deeper voice, a little mustache and a little grass around my redwood. But Summer had grown a lot, especially over this past summer. She had grown into a b-cup. Her hips were a little wider and her butt a little bigger. Her former curly brown hair was now straight and hung just below her shoulders. Her sexy brown eyes put me in a trance. And her soft pink lips would open up into a smile that

was brighter than the sun. I
couldn't help but be in awe of her.

"Where you want to go?" I
asked not really caring where we
went as long as we were together.

Summer thought to herself for
a minute. "I'm kind of in the mood
for a Casper's dog."

I had to admit I was in love
with Casper's Dogs. The Caspers on
51st and Telegraph was one of our
hangout spots. Eric, Natalie,
Summer and I would ride our bikes
almost every Saturday when it
wasn't raining or Eric didn't have a
basketball game. It was a way to get
full for cheap and feel independent
from our parents. Since we all had
licenses, we seem to hardly have
time to go to our hangout spot
together. Summer was the only one
of us who didn't have a license.

"That's cool, let me just finish
drying the car and I'll take you."

Summer puts her hands on her
hips, "You gonna pay for me?"

I looked at her like she was
crazy. "Why do I have to pay for
you?" But at the same time I was
thinking that I would pay for
anything for her.

"Well, it's just the two of us and
you're the boy so you should pay."

I scratch my head, trying to figure out if she was saying this trip to Caspers was a date. "But it's not like we're boyfriend and girlfriend." I tell her trying to figure out her angle.

Summer puts her hands into the pockets of her yellow shorts. My eyes focus on her developing breasts through her yellow, red and white stripped tank top. I thought about how soft they were and what would happen to her when I rubbed them. I start to rise and quickly try to hold my dry towel in front of me. Just thinking about Summer made me crazy. And after four years and three girlfriends, she was still the only girl to ever let me feel her up. Our relationship was special that way.

Summer breaks my train of thought. "We could be boyfriend and girlfriend."

I look at her to see if she's joking or being serious. She avoids eye contact so she must be serious. I can't believe she actually just said that. All this time I thought she just used me to experiment with. I never thought she actually wanted to be my girlfriend.

133

I finish drying the car and walk to her. "You always said you want to keep it as just friends who kissed sometimes."

Summer takes her hands out of pockets and folds them then shifts her weight to one leg. "Yeah, well, when you broke up with Tenese last month I thought maybe you would have thought about us. I mean since you broke up with her, we've been sneaking off to kiss even more. I even let you touch me all over."

I did just break up with Tenese after a three week relationship. I hadn't tried more with Summer because she had a guy after her. And not that I'm scary, but Summer's crush was almost six foot and one-eighty. He also played on the football and basketball teams. I really wasn't trying to be on his bad side.

"Well what about you and Chris?"

She sucks her teeth. "I told you he is not my boyfriend. He wants to be but.... Never mind, forget I said something."

Summer tries to walk away. I grab her arm and turn her to face me. I look at her. She's still the most beautiful girl I had ever seen in my life. Her big brown eyes stare into mine. I lean in and kiss her as if for the first time. It just felt different, like there was more feeling, more passion, more love.

Summer looks at me and smiles. "So does this mean you're paying?"

I smile and kiss her again, this time just a peck. "Come on, let's go eat."

That was the summer we made it official. We were boyfriend and girlfriend, but by the time school started in September, we had broken up. She started dating Chris and I was getting girls numbers left and right. The only problem was that none of them stuck because I wanted to be with Summer. But she stayed with Chris all of Junior year and most of Senior year. I don't know what it is about the jocks but they always seem to get the finest girls in school. I didn't do so bad but being a photographer wasn't considered as tough as playing football. But the girls did love for me to take their pictures.

Thinking back to that summer, that was the only time Summer and I actually called each other boyfriend and girlfriend, but it was definitely not the last time we were intimate. We didn't even have sex during that time. She always said she was saving herself for marriage. But like Eric always said, every girl is saving herself until you get her to the bedroom. I just never wanted to pressure her. After we broke up, I never thought I would have sex with Summer. I would have regretted never sleeping with her.

"Are you alright?" Alexis breaks my daydream.

"Yeah I'm fine." I try to assure her, hoping she couldn't tell I was thinking of another woman.

Alexis takes my hand as we continue to walk towards my car. "What's on your mind, Sean?"

"Just thinking about the past. Growing up here. Feels weird to be visiting Oakland when I still consider it my home." This wasn't a lie. All of my childhood memories are in Oakland. And my best childhood memories included Summer.

Alexis stops walking and looks at me. "Do you want to move back here?"

I shake my head no. "Our work is in LA," I know I wouldn't be

making as much money here in
Oakland as I would in Los Angeles.

"You left a lot of things here in
Oakland."

I can tell Alexis means
Summer. She's thinking that
Summer is the one thing I'm
missing in my life. I have to let
Alexis know I love her and I do want
to marry her. I don't want to make
her feel insecure.

"But I found the best things in
LA," I tell her in all seriousness.

Alexis kisses me. She takes my
hand and we continue walking. "So
tell me all about you growing up
here."

Chapter 9

Sean

We get back to the car and drive to Emeryville where Natalie is setting up her new store in the Bay Street Shopping Center, an outside strip mall. I tell Alexis how back in day the biggest attraction to Emeryville was the Public Market, which was a short distance from where the Bay Street Shopping Center is. You can buy food from almost every culture on earth at the Public Market. In just over ten or so years, more stores have popped up and have made the once quiet town of Emeryville a busy consumer town. I used to think of Emeryville as just an extension of Oakland, but it's proving to be a thriving town in it's own right.

I park in the huge parking garage on the third level, put the alarm on my car and take Alexis by the hand. She intertwines her soft

138

smooth fingers with mine. Just her touch makes me feel nervous and excited at the same time. I'm totally in love with Alexis. But I still can't stop thinking about Summer. Knowing the friendship Natalie and Summer have, Summer is probably in the store helping Natalie set up. I know I told Summer I would meet her here this afternoon but now I'm thinking that it may be a bad idea.

Alexis has just shown me she is still insecure about Summer. I wonder if once she sees Summer would she then think Summer is better looking, smarter, or sexier than she is. Not that Alexis has anything to worry about, I mean, she is a model and her body is beyond sexy.

I begin to get a little anxious as Alexis and I walk down the street towards Natalie's store. I get hot. My hands start sweating. I start feeling sick to my stomach. Alexis must see the nervousness on my face. Either that or she can just tell I'm not feeling right.

"You okay, Sean?"

I stop and look at her but can't speak.

"What's wrong, Baby?" She
puts her hand on my head trying to
see if I have a temperature.

I close my eyes and think about
Summer. When I walk into the
store and see her, what's going to
happen? Will it be awkward? Will
she run to me and kiss me and tell
me how much she misses me and
still loves me? Will she tell me she
was sorry for not fighting harder to
make our relationship work and
that I'm the only man for her? Will
she tell me to dump Alexis and
marry her?

"Sean!"

Alexis interrupts my near
nervous breakdown.

"I'm good." I lie. I lie to protect
her feelings, I think. Maybe I lied to
keep my true feelings from coming
out?

Alexis takes both my hands in
hers and looks me in the eye.

"I know. Don't feel nervous."

What does she mean she
knows? Does she know about the
phone calls from Summer? I know
the walls are thin at my parents
place but I tried to talk as low as
possible. Does she know Summer
and I set up a meeting today? I
close my eyes again trying to block

all of these crazy thoughts that are
swarming through my mind. I open
my eyes and look at Alexis and
smile. She kisses me on the lips
and I feel my anxiety rush out of my
body. I nod, put my arm around her
and we walk down a few stores until
we get to Natalie's Boutique. I'm
ready to take on what ever comes
my way. It's finally time to confront
Summer and my feelings.

I look at the store and the first
thing I notice is the black paper
covering the inside of the windows
so you can't see in. On the outside
of the windows are two huge signs
that say "Grand Opening Saturday
at 3 PM." I try to open the door but
it's locked. I knock three times,
hard. A few seconds later I hear the
keys rattle and the door is unlocked
and opened. Alexis and I walk in,
and the young lady who opened the
door closes it and locks it back with
her key.

I look around the small
boutique. It has bright vivid colors
on the walls, which makes me feel at
peace. The smell of incense fills the
air. I look to the left where Natalie
has an assortment of classy evening
gowns and dresses, some on the
racks while others were on well

141

placed all black mannequins. To the right of the store are more casual wear, jeans and T-shirts . Towards the back of the store are several rows of shoes ranging from high heels, to boots, to tennis shoes and everything in between. In the center of the store are small glass cases with hand made jewelry. Next to the glass case are two wooden stands with cash registers on them. Behind one of the cash registers stands Natalie.

Natalie is and has always been a beautiful black sista. Her deep dark skin looks smooth and flawless. She wears jeans that hug her hips and thighs and make her ass look picture perfect. Her white top shows her double d cleavage. A white and pink A's baseball cap covers her short black hair and hides her small brown eyes.

"I knew that was you. Where have you been? I've been waiting on you for 2 hours."

The young lady who opened the door walks to Natalie and gives her the key. She then walks to the back of the store to arrange some of the shoes.

Alexis and I walk to the register where Natalie greets me with a hug and kiss on the cheek.

"You went over to see Eric first, didn't you?"

I nod. Natalie shakes her head at me. Natalie and I were friends on the block first. For about two years, we were the only kids on the block. Then when Eric moved to 44th Street, things changed. Eric and Natalie were constantly getting into arguments and they just seemed to not like each other at all. They still seem to argue about the dumbest things even to this day. But they always have each other's back no matter what. They're like brother and sister. The same goes for me and Natalie, although we never seem to argue. Truth be told, she scared me a little. I saw her put Eric in a headlock once when we were kids and he complained of pain for two weeks.

"So this is Alexis, the model and dancer I've heard so much about?"

Alexis extends her hand. Natalie moves the hand and gives Alexis a huge hug. She's always been big on hugs and I have to admit you felt warm after getting a

143

hug from Natalie. You also always wanted to stay on Natalie's good side because just as good as it felt to get a hug from Natalie, it felt just as bad to feel her wrath.

"You finally get to meet her." I tell her, happy to see that Alexis is doing great with my family and friends. They all seem to like her at first glance. She doesn't need to say a word, they just love her.

Natalie releases the hug and looks at Alexis and smiles. She then looks at me.

"Those magazines and video's don't do you justice girl. You're much prettier in person," Natalie turns to me, "She actually looks like she's too good for you."

We all laugh.

"I think we're just right for each other." Alexis says as she interlocks her arm with mine.

"Aww, Sean you got the girl brain washed."

We all laugh again.

I look around for a few seconds to see if Summer is here. I don't see her. My eyes lock on Natalie and she rolls her eyes. Natalie then looks at Alexis.

"So, Alexis, I know this is short notice but since you're a model and

I am doing a fashion show for my opening tomorrow night, would you be willing to model a dress or two?" Natalie asks.

I answer before Alexis can. "Nat, she's a print model not a runway model, and plus she's here visiting not working."

Alexis takes her arm from mine and puts her hands on her hips. "What are you saying? I can't make it on the cat walk?"

Alexis does a model strut like she's been doing it for years. I had never actually seen her do that. The way she moved her hips made me think about how she moves them in bed. I begin to get a little aroused. She is so sexy and at times I can't believe she's all mine. I try to keep my arousal at bay so I try to think of other things. But the only other thing I can think of is Summer.

Alexis makes her way back to me and Natalie. Natalie gives Alexis a hi-five. Alexis looks at me as if to say what do think about that Mr. Winters. I think I want to see you do that tonight when we're alone.

"Well then I guess it's settled. Alexis will be modeling." Natalie doesn't need Alexis to say yes or no, the walk Alexis just did was all the answer Natalie needed. "Come on, girl, let me show you the dresses I want you to wear."

Alexis gives me a peck on the cheek and follows Natalie to the back. I watch her walk away and think of how great her ass looks in those jeans. I walk around the store for a few seconds just looking at the different clothes my friend has designed. I stop at a dress. It's not just any dress, it's the same dress Summer wore when we went to prom.

"Look familiar." A sexy voice says from behind me. I don't need to turn around to know it's Summer.

"Yeah, it's the dress you wore the first time we..."

Summer turns me around. I'm speechless. She looks better than I can remember. She cut her brown hair to just above her shoulders. Her b-cup has grown into a c-cup and she's carrying a little something extra in her backside. I'm intoxicated with her perfume. It feels like I'm on a love high. Summer stands in front of me wearing a short grey dress with a huge black belt and black boots.

"Don't say that out loud." She says with a giggle.

Her sexy brown eyes make me follow her every word. I want to kiss her pink lips which are glazed with lip-gloss.

"But yes, that is the dress Natalie made ten years ago for prom. A few updates but that's the one."

"It still looks good. You still look good."

I wrap my arms around her and she hugs me back for what seems like forever. I am in love with the way she smells, the way she looks and the way she feels at this moment.

Summer breaks the hug. "Thanks, Honey, you still look good yourself."

"How you been?" I ask trying to see if Alexis is coming my way while wondering if Alexis and Summer had just crossed paths.

"I've been good." She says in a sexy voice. I can smell the watermelon gum coming off of her breath. I inhale it as if it's the sweetest smell.

She brushes her hair behind her ear and lets her hand rest on her neck. She looks at me and

smiles and I know I'm in trouble.
Not because I have done something
wrong but because I'm ready to do
something wrong.

"So, I don't see your girlfriend,
did you come alone?" She asks with
bit of hope in her tone.

"She went to the back with
Natalie. She's trying on some
clothes that Nat wants her to model
for tomorrow night."

I can see disappointment on
her face. Summer wanted me to tell
her yes I left Alexis at home so that
we can have some alone time. But
that wasn't the case. If Summer
had something to say, she needs to
say it right now or forever hold her
peace. And everything I have to say
needs to be said right now. There's
no backing down now. We're here
and we need to have closure.

"I must have missed her. I was
just using the rest room."

I want us to get everything off
of our chest before Alexis comes
back so I press the issue. "So what
did you need to talk to me about?"

She sucks her teeth and puts
her hands on her hips obviously
annoyed that I seem to be rushing
her. "Look, Sean, I just wanted to

tell you that I've been thinking about you, us a lot lately."

Okay, here it goes. She's about to let all of her feelings out. I have to stay strong and not give in to the temptation. But I don't think I can. If Summer asks me to come back to her place, then Alexis is going to have to find a way to my parent's place or to the nearest airport. I don't think I'm strong enough to say no to Summer. I have to keep telling myself to stay strong.

"Hey Sean." I hear a familiar voice calling out my name. I look to the side and see Krystal coming from the back of the store.

Krystal, Eric's girlfriend waddles towards us. She's about seven months pregnant and is glowing. I don't know why but pregnant women are beautiful. Maybe it's because of the new life that they are carrying inside them. Krystal looks good in her white sweats and pink maternity shirt. I smile because she has a giant bag of potato chips in her hand.

I give her a big hug. "Hey, Krystal. How are you?"

"I'm good. I'm ready to drop this baby."

"You're looking good," Summer says, a little ticked off because Krystal interrupted our conversation.

"Thanks, Summer. I don't feel it though." Krystal turns her attention to me. "Now that girl you're about to marry, she looks good."

Summer rolls her eyes. I try to say something but she just walks away to the back of the store and begins talking to the girl that opened the door for us. Now I'm the one mad. I can't believe Krystal just blurted out that I'm engaged in front of Summer. That was not the way I wanted her to find out.

"So you met Alexis?"

"Oh, yeah and she's a ten. You always did have some good looking women." Krystal says as she devours another chip.

"So you and Eric getting married anytime soon?" I know that was a cheap shot, but she did just mess up a chance with Summer, if I had a chance. I guess now I'll never know.

Krystal looks at me with disgust. "You know your boy is never going to put a ring on my finger. I've been waiting five years

150

and all he's done is get me
pregnant."

"Now after five years, how does
he get you pregnant?" I ask,
wondering if she was like a bunch of
other women I've met. They get
pregnant in hopes the father of the
child will settle down and marry
them.

"What you trying to say, Sean?
You think I trapped him?" She's
getting a little irritated at me. Good.
She shouldn't have opened her
mouth about my engagement.

"I'm just asking?" I tell her
with a smirk on my face. A piece of
me wanted her to admit that she got
pregnant on purpose.

"Well, how did you and
Summer sleep together for so long
and you not get her pregnant? Or
Alexis, you've been with her for two
years and you haven't got her
pregnant."

What she didn't realize was
Summer had gotten pregnant once
but we never told anybody. She had
an abortion before anyone could
notice. We never spoke of it. It
didn't stop us from sleeping
together. It just made us become
more careful.

"I just thought you guys were always careful. I mean you're the one that always said marriage before baby."

"Let's just say, things happen, Sean." Krystal says still snacking on her chips.

Alexis and Natalie come from the back room where I assume Natalie has her office and possibly dressing rooms since I don't see any out in the store. The two are talking and laughing like they have been friends for years.

"Sean, Alexis is too funny." Natalie says as they make it to me and Krystal.

"No she's the funny one. She was telling me about the time she had to beat you up." Alexis says trying to hold in her laughter.

I try to defend myself. "She didn't beat me up. She just hit me and I didn't hit her back."

"That's not the story Eric told me." Krystal says sucking the crumbs and grease from the chips off of her fingers.

"Now you know the only reason you didn't hit me back was because you couldn't get up." Natalie holds her stomach. "He was like, I can't breath, I can't breath."

They all start laughing.

I start to get a little embarrassed. How is Alexis going to look at me now, knowing that Natalie once punched me in the stomach so hard she knocked the wind out of me? Eric talked about me for a month after that happened. I mean, it was my fault; I shouldn't have been joking about her hair. But in all honesty, on that day, her hair looked like she had just been through a tornado.

Alexis sees I'm getting a little frustrated. She walks over and puts her arms around me. "It's okay, Baby, you got rock hard ABS now. You could take a punch." Alexis says as she pats my abdomen.

"Don't try and pump up his ego." Natalie says, "He knows he's never been a fighter."

Alexis kisses me on the cheek. "I know you can protect me, Baby."

Now I'm feeling like I have to do something to show my masculinity. Like maybe Picking Krystal's pregnant self up. Or trying to bench-press Alexis. I know Alexis just said she knows I'm strong now but a piece of her is always going to remember that I was beat up by a girl before. I've tried to forget that incident ever since I was thirteen.

It was a hot summer day in July. I had just got my first camera the week before on my birthday. I was using Summer and Eric as models. I had set up different poses in my parents driveway and on our red cement steps. The shots were coming out great. Then here comes Natalie.

I was just finishing a pose of Eric and Summer standing back to back on the steps. Natalie walks up and we all start laughing. Her hair was everywhere. Of course she didn't know what the big deal was at first.

"What y'all doing? What's so funny?"

Of course Eric points out the obvious. "Girl, your hair looks like somebody just tried to use a vacuum cleaner on it."

We all start laughing again. Natalie, a little embarrassed puts her hand to her hair.

Sweet Summer tries to help. "It's not that bad. "

Of course I had to open my mouth and say, "Don't lie to her Summer."

Natalie pushes me. "Leave me alone before I hurt you."

"Don't mess with her, Sean, you see what she did to her hair. Who knows what she'll do to you." Eric says trying hard not to laugh. He failed.

"Whatever four eyes." Natalie turns her attention to me. "Why you didn't tell me you were taking pictures? I want to be in some."

I didn't want to say it, it just came out. "You can be in the pictures after you go and get your hair done."

Next thing I know Natalie punches me hard in the stomach and knocks me to the ground. Luckily I didn't drop the camera but I did drop any self-respect I had. I couldn't breathe; I tried gasping for air but couldn't get it. I look up and Eric and Summer are no longer laughing at Natalie but with Natalie at me. That was probably the most embarrassing moment of my life. Now I'm standing here with my fiancée feeling even more embarrassed. Luckily Krystal changes the subject.

"Hey, Nat, you need me for anything else, cause I need to get over to the club and help Eric."

"You're good, Krystal. Go help that slow boy. Lord knows he needs it." Natalie tells her.

Krystal extends her clean hand to Alexis. "It was nice meeting you."

Alexis hugs Krystal instead. "Nice meeting you too."

Krystal and Natalie walk to the front door where Natalie unlocks the door and lets Krystal out, then closes and locks the door behind her.

Alexis whispers in my ear. "Your friends are really nice."

"That's only because you don't know them that well." I joke.

I know my friends are cool. I just hate I don't get to see or talk to them as much anymore. We are all so busy nowadays and with me living in LA, it's impossible for us all to be around each other at once. I still talk to Eric and Natalie at least once a week but it's not the same. We use to see each other everyday, now the only time I see them is when I have business here in the Bay and even that doesn't always happen.

Natalie walks back to us. "So what do you guys think about the store?"

I give Natalie a hug and tell her I'm proud of her. When I release the hug I see Summer coming our way. I look over at Alexis who sees what I see. Natalie turns around as Summer makes it to us. It feels extremely awkward. I'm not sure what's about to happen. A piece of me wants to see Summer and Alexis fight. Two women fighting over me would be sexy as hell. But in my world that doesn't happen.

Summer extends her hand to Alexis. "Hi, you must be Alexis."

Alexis shakes Summer's hand. "Yes and you must be Summer."

Summer nods as they release the handshake. "I just wanted to come over and congratulate you and Sean on your engagement."

Alexis smiles and walks to me. "Thank you. It just happened yesterday and we're excited."

Summer looks at me and sees the worried look on my face. "I can tell."

For the first time I'm looking at the two women who have a piece of my heart trying to figure out who has the bigger piece. For the first time I am not comparing Alexis to Summer but rather Summer to Alexis. Summer at the moment almost seems fake. It's like she's putting on a show, acting like she's happy for me when really she wants me back. I'm not sure if I want her back at this moment.

Alexis, in a polite way is marking her territory. She has every right to do so. She is wearing my ring. But I can also tell Alexis is showing some insecurities. She's looking Summer up and down to see what I loved about her. Summer doesn't have the legs that Alexis has and Summer is about five inches shorter although her heels give her some height. Summer is a little thicker in the right places and Summer has prettier eyes.

I see Summer looking at Alexis trying to check out the competition. Trying to figure out why after so many years and so many women, Alexis is the one that stopped our friends with benefits relationship. Summer sees Alexis as the woman who stole her one reliable lover. Summer has dealt with men who cheated on her, beat on her, and used her. But me, I would never do that to her and I think she realized it too late.

I'm stuck speechless. I don't know what to say. Alexis has

already given me permission to talk
to Summer and see where we stand.
But now that Summer knows I'm
engaged, I doubt she would be
willing to put her feelings on the line
in fear of getting hurt for no reason.
But I need to know what's on her
mind. Why did she call me last
night? Why did she want to talk to
me so bad? Why does she miss me?
Does she want me back? These are
questions I need answered before I
can fully commit to Alexis.

Natalie tries to break the
tension. "Summer did you finish
making sure everything was
arranged properly?"

Summer takes a second to
respond. She finally looks at
Natalie. "Yes, Nat, everything is
perfect for tomorrow."

"Good. And you have the
dresses you'll be modeling
tomorrow?" Natalie asks Summer.

"Yes."

Alexis speaks up. "You're
modeling too? Natalie just asked me
to model for her tomorrow as well."

Summer gives Alexis a fake
smile. "See you tomorrow, then."
Summer winks in our direction and
walks away.

Natalie looks at me and gives me a motherly look. I know what it means. She's telling me not to ruin her grand opening tomorrow. I don't want to ruin it and maybe she should be telling Summer the same thing. After all, she called me and wanted to talk.

I look at Alexis who looks at me. I can tell what's on her mind as well. It's the same thing on my mind. The wink Summer just gave, was that for her or was it for me?

Chapter 10

Summer

I slam my hand down on the bathroom sink. "Damn."

I can't believe he's engaged. This changes everything. Sean must really love this girl if he put that rock on her finger. I've gotten bigger rings from men wanting to wife me but they didn't really love me. They just wanted a trophy wife on their arm and felt that the big ring guaranteed I would be there no matter what. Even if they slept around or beat me. Or both.

"What am I supposed to do now?"

I'm trying to fight back tears. It's hard because I feel my heart breaking. The one man I love and want to be with is getting married. And Alexis seems like a good woman. Maybe Sean is gone for good. Maybe Alexis got what I was too blind to see or too slow to get.

But I should be the one marrying Sean.

I think back to five years ago when I found out I was pregnant. I had just gone through a bad break up and Sean comforted me. I flew to LA to be with him and we made love for an entire weekend. I didn't make him go buy condoms. I just wanted to feel him inside me. A few weeks later, I found out I was pregnant and it was his. He seemed like he wanted to keep it but I didn't want to mess up my chances at finishing medical school. He reluctantly wired me some money and I got the abortion. I haven't regretted that decision until now. Knowing the man Sean is, had I kept the baby he, would have married me and Alexis would have never come into the picture.

"I can't lose Sean. Maybe if we do have time to talk alone, he'll see he still loves me and drop Alexis."

I had so many things I wanted to say to Sean but didn't have the opportunity. Krystal just had to come over and interrupt with her pregnant ass. She stopped me from telling Sean that I love him and have always loved him. I needed to apologize for not seeing it sooner. I wanted to tell him I made a mistake leaving him for another man. I only did it because I knew if things didn't work out I could always come back to him. But that wasn't the case.

Sean never complained when I met someone new and wanted to be monogamous with that person. Hell it always seemed as if he had a girl or two waiting in the wings. But whenever I broke up with a guy and went back to Sean, he would always drop those other girls quick and just be with me. That is, until Alexis.

I was really hoping Alexis would be unattractive. Of course I had seen Alexis in some magazines and music video's, but with the right make-up team you can make anyone look sexy on camera. But even with the little make-up Alexis was wearing today, she looked beautiful. And, Alexis seems to be what I failed to be, loyal to Sean.

I have to face the fact that Sean may be gone from me forever. Time to go back out to the store and help Natalie finish setting up. I adjust my dress and make sure my make-up still looks good. I don't want to walk back out to Natalie's store looking sad or depressed. I open the bathroom door and head to the front area of the store. I barely take two steps before Natalie comes out of nowhere and grabs me by the arm.

"Nat, what the hell?"

Natalie leads me into her small office and closes the door. She releases the hold she has on my arm and just stares at me for what seems like forever. I rub my arm all while wondering what was Natalie's problem. She had no right to grab me the way she did and drag me in here like I was her child. I want to push or slap her but I know better, Natalie would have whooped my ass in two point five seconds.

"Don't think I didn't see that wink." Natalie finally says, looking like a mother about to chastise her child.

"You trippin, Nat."

"I told you to let Sean be. He's got a good woman. Don't mess it up for him."

I just smile at her. I don't want her to see the hurt in my eyes. "All I did was congratulate him on his engagement."

Natalie folds her arms. "Don't nobody believe that fake congratulations."

"Whatever." I roll my eyes and try to head for the door but Natalie blocks my path. "Come on, Nat, let me out."

"Summer, I'm telling you to let it go. Please."

I look at my best friend and wonder why she isn't on my side right now. Why doesn't Natalie want me to fight for Sean? Doesn't she believe in true love? Natalie is the one who is married. And she married Charles after fighting her feelings for another man. Now she's happy and all because she didn't give up on her one true love.

"Natalie, I love him. Can't you see that?"

"I love Sean too, but I'm not in love with him, and I don't think you are either."

I'm shocked by Natalie's statement. How would she know if I was in love with Sean or not? She doesn't know my heart like I do. I know now that I've been in love with Sean since high school. I just never accepted it. Now that I'm older and have had some bad relationships, I know Sean is the man for me. Sean would never cheat on me. He would never use or abuse me. He would never break my heart.

"I am in love with Sean."

Natalie shakes her head. "You're not in love with him. You're just horny and he's your safety net."

There's a knock on the door. The door opens and in walks Charles, Natalie's husband. He's the total opposite of what you would expect Natalie to end up with. He's about an inch shorter than her, very thin and he's a computer geek. He makes pretty good money, doing IT work for Kaiser Permanente's home office in Downtown Oakland. And from what Natalie says, he's a beast in bed. He's also one of the few guys I know that isn't scared of Natalie.

"Hey, sorry for interrupting, I got off work early and wanted to see if you needed some help setting up."

Natalie walks to her husband and gives him a kiss. "We're pretty much finished, but, if you want, you can go get us a table at the Elephant Bar and I'll be there in a few minutes."

"Sounds good." Charles and Natalie kiss again, with more passion. Charles exits the office closing the door behind him.

Natalie turns around with a huge smile on her face like she's on cloud nine. It disgusts me at the moment. Why does she get to be happy and I don't? I deserve a good man like her. Sean is that good man and right now Natalie is blocking. She's not going to win this fight. I know Natalie is tough, but even she can't beat up destiny. And Sean and I are destined to be together.

"So, what is it? You're the only one that can be happy?" It felt good to break her love high.

"It's not that I don't want you to be happy but I want Sean to be happy too."

"And you don't think he would be happy with me?"

Natalie shakes her head. "No, because in the end, I don't think you would make him happy."

Now she's pissing me off. "How can you say that? I'm your best friend."

"That's how I can say it. Because I'm your best friend. Summer you need to figure out what you want in a relationship before you try to jump into another one. Sean figured that out. That's why he's happy with Alexis."

"Are we done?" I need to leave the room before I start crying like a baby.

"Yeah, we're done."

I walk for the door. "I'll see you tomorrow."

I walk out of the office and out of the back door of the store as quick as I can. My mind is racing thinking about what Natalie just told me. How dare she tell me I wouldn't make Sean happy? Every time we were together he was happy. I always gave him the goods the way he liked. Sean couldn't ask for a better lover. I was his first everything, including his first lingerie model. And I know I can cook better than Alexis. Sean never complained about my cooking. I kept him fed and satisfied. And Natalie has the nerve to say I wouldn't make Sean happy?

"What does she know?"

As I walk to towards the parking garage, I think about what I want in a relationship. I want what every girl wants. Love, honesty, respect and loyalty. Sean has all those qualities and more. He looks good. He's successful and he has his own home. What more can a girl ask for? Natalie is wrong. I am not going to let Sean go without a fight. I'm going to get Sean back, tonight.

Chapter 11

Sean

After doing a little shopping and stopping by Cold Stone, Alexis and I make it back to the car and out the parking garage without saying anything to each other. I can tell she has a lot on her mind but she can't find the right words to say. I know what's on my mind, Summer. She looked good and smelled better. I wanted to stay there and be intoxicated by every bit of her. I wanted to get a love high so great I'd become a junkie for it. I wanted to take Summer somewhere and just sex her crazy like we used to do. But I can't do any of those things because I am committed to Alexis.

"So, Summer is cute."

Alexis catches me of guard. I was expecting her to trash talk Summer but instead she gave her a compliment. I don't know if this is a trick to get me to say something incriminating about Summer.

"I mean, I can see why you were with her." Alexis says looking at me for a reaction.

"Yeah, she is cute, I guess."

Alexis laughs. "You guess. Come on now, Sean, you can't sleep with a girl for years and just guess she's cute."

I knew it. This was a trick. Alexis wants to know how I feel now that I've seen Summer. The truth is, I don't know. We really didn't get a chance to talk and all I could think about was how much I wanted to get inside of her. That's just my normal attraction to Summer. I've wanted to sleep with her since we were kids and when it finally happened, I wanted to do it over and over and over again. Nothing in the world felt better than being with Summer, that is, until I met Alexis. Now Summer may have been wilder in bed than Alexis, but Summer didn't always take the time to please me in every way. Sex with Summer was always all about her, but I didn't care as long as I was inside of her.

"You still want to be with her, don't you?" Alexis asks as I make a

left on San Pablo heading towards
Forty-Third Street.

"Why do you keep asking me
that?" I ask trying to get to the root
of her insecurity, because now it's
starting to annoy me.

"You're the one who said you
weren't sure if you still had feelings
for Summer. What? I'm supposed to
just except that?"

I park on the street in front of
my parents house and stay silent. I
don't really know what to say but I
have to get Alexis off of my back
about Summer. I've tried and tried
to make Alexis see that I love her
and want to be with her but she
keeps bringing up my feelings for
Summer. It's almost like if I go and
cheat then that would satisfy her.
It's as if she's expecting me to cheat.
So, why not do it? To her I already
cheated when I told her I wasn't
sure about my feelings for Summer.
So if she already thinks I'm cheating
in my heart, why not do the
physical? It won't change anything.

She speaks, her voice calm.
"Sean, I just want to know if I have
anything to worry about. I've been
hurt before and I need to know that
you're not going to hurt me too."

I look at Alexis trying to find the right words to say but I choose the wrong ones. "For the past two years I've tried to show you I'm not like the other men in your life, but you don't believe me when I tell you that I only want you. So you know what? Until you can trust me, maybe you should give that ring back because I can't be with you if you don't trust me."

There is a long, cold, tense silence in the car. Alexis looks at her ring. I look at her trying to figure out what's going on in her mind. She probably wants to curse me out, yell at me, hit me, throw things, maybe even tear up my car. I didn't want to say it. But, how many times can I tell her I'm not cheating and I'm not going to cheat before it becomes annoying and too much? I asked her to marry me because I knew right then that she was the one woman I wanted to spend the rest of my life with. But her constant nagging has got me thinking that Summer may be the better choice. Alexis needs to make the decision of whether she can trust me or not. If she can't trust me, then we don't need to be together.

A knock on the window breaks our silence. It's Andrea standing on the passenger side with a big smile on her face. I roll the window down to see what my little sister wants.

"Hey, I hope I'm not interrupting anything, but I saw the car." She says still smiling big.

"What's up, Drea?" I ask with a little attitude.

"I just thought that since you guys are back, Alexis could help with that one move I can't seem to get."

I start to tell Andrea to come back another time but Alexis cuts me off and opens the car door and gets out.

"Come on, Andrea, lets go practice."

Alexis slams the car door and walks away without looking back at me. I just sit in the car thinking, but not about Alexis, about Summer. I'm trying to be a good, stand-up man and not go after Summer, but she looked so damn good today. It took everything in me not to try and leave with her today. But the way Alexis is acting right now, it would be better if I go after Summer. She's the one who wants me to confront my feelings and her

173

questions won't quiet down unless I can honestly answer them all.

I pull out my phone and call Summer. She answers on the second ring.

"What's up, Sean?" The tone of her voice has changed from sweet to annoyed. She didn't even call me honey.

"You busy right now?" I ask hoping she would say no.

"I just finished with Nat. Why?" She knows why and she's going to make me work for it now.

"I need to talk with you. We didn't finish our conversation earlier."

There's a long pause before she answers. "There's nothing to talk about. You're getting married. That's all I need to know."

"What if there is more you need to know?"

Summer sighs and sucks her teeth. "Fine, Sean, meet me in about a half hour. I live off of Broadway Terrace, across from the Claremont golf course."

"Yeah, I know where that is. I'll be there."

"I'll see you in a bit, Honey."

We hang-up. I look back at my parents' place and see The Good

174

Reverend Winters coming my way. I begin to start the car up and drive away but I decide against it. Without asking, my father opens the passenger door and sits.

"What's the problem, son?" He asks in a concerned voice. It irritates me.

"Nothing, I'm fine." I tell him hoping he would get out my car.

"Well, you have a good looking woman inside. Your mother made your favorite meal and you're sitting in the car looking like you've just got a call to deploy."

"You wouldn't understand."

After saying that, I want to take it back because he would probably understand. He was once caught up between two women and although I think he made the wrong choice, something good came out of it, my little sister. But do I really want to ask my father for advice? It would be like asking the enemy for help. I shouldn't feel that way but I do.

"You never talk to me, Sean. I know I've made some mistakes, but everyone has seemed to have forgiven me but you."

I wish I could forgive him but he nearly destroyed our family. He embarrassed us before the church and our family and friends. He made my mother raise a child that wasn't hers. He made me a target for jokes at school. And above all, he never apologized to me for all he put us through.

"You've never asked me for forgiveness." I tell him.

He looks at me for a second, but doesn't say anything. He's probably trying to think back to all the people he's apologized to over the years and trying to find when he apologized to me. He won't find a time because there isn't one. I guess he just figured I'd fall in line with my mother and just act like it never happened. But I know it happened. I'm reminded every time I think about Andrea and how she got here.

"Sean, I'm sorry, I never thought about it I guess." He says, trying to be sincere.

"It's too late now, I shouldn't have had to tell you. Now if you would excuse me I'm going to take a drive." I tell him trying to get him out of my car.

He looks at me, then nods. He uses his cane to help him up and starts to close the car door. "I've been where you're at, Sean. Don't make my mistakes." He says as he closes the door and walks back to the house.

I roll down the window. "Tell mom to save me a plate. I'll be back in a while." He nods but doesn't turn around. I start up my car and head towards Broadway Terrace.

Chapter 12

Alexis

Andrea and I practice the praise dance downstairs in the small apartment. It's taken a minute but Andrea finally has the spin down. She seems to appreciate the time and patience I'm giving her and after about the fifth try, she finally got it. We both sit on the bed, sweaty and tired from dancing. The music still plays in the background as we try to relax. Andrea brought a bottle of water for us and I am enjoying a drink as it cools down my body.

"So what's it like dancing in music videos?" Andrea asks excitedly.

"It's hard work and you have to be selective in the projects you choose."

"What do you mean?"

"I never wanted to be just one of the booty shaking girls. I always chose my projects based on my role in the video. I was either a love interest or I was doing real choreographed dancing. Because choreographed dancing tells a story, booty shaking doesn't."

Andrea looks at me like she's the student and I'm the master. I feel like I have to tell her the truth so she doesn't end up like a bunch of girls I know. They get caught up in the life of hanging with stars and the glitz and glamour of it all. I've known too many good girls who got turned out and I was not going to be one of them. I notice a frown take over Andrea's face. "What's wrong?"

"Ever since I was a little girl, all I've ever wanted to do was be a dancer." She tells me. Her eyes stare into space. I imagine that she is thinking of the first time she discovered her love for dance. Then she looks down to her hands. "Dad just thinks it's a hobby. He's pushing me to be a business major."

I place my hand on her cheek and slowly guide her to look at me. I notice her eyes watering. Not enough to produce tears, but enough to give her a glassy look. I can tell she's in a battle. On one hand, she wants to make her father happy. But on the other, she wants to follow her heart and dance. She wants both hands to come together and shake in agreement. She wants to dance and she wants her father to be proud of that. I believe she should be able to do what she's passionate about. "What do you want to do?"

"I got accepted into San Francisco State University and they have a good dance program. But like I said, my dad wants me to focus on business." Andrea tells me with disappointment in her voice.

"Why not do both? I mean you can do a double major or major in one and minor in the other?"

Andrea shakes her head. "My dad doesn't think dance is reliable."

I smile. That's the same thing my big sister told me. "That's not true. I'm very successful. I bring home close to a thousand dollars a week teaching dance classes. Even more if I'm doing private lessons. To do a video makes me a little more depending on the project. And if I'm choreographing a video or stage performance, we're talking big money."

Andrea gets an excited look on her face but it disappears. "Dad won't go for it. Mom would though.

She's been encouraging me to dance since I was five. But dad controls the money. He say's if he's paying for college, I have to major in what he wants me to major in. It's not fair!" She stands, folds her arms and pouts.

I can sense Andrea's frustration and I want to help. Maybe God has me here this weekend to help both Sean and Andrea get things right with their father. I've been where Andrea is. When I called and asked my sister for money to move to LA so I could become a dancer, she flat out told me no. She could have helped. She told me if I went to LA, the only dancing I would be doing is in a strip club. It's a good thing my Aunt believed in me and got me to LA and into an apartment with my cousin Simone.

I know Andrea feels she has to do what her father wants her to do. But I also know true happiness comes from doing what makes you happy, not what makes others happy. I knew I wanted to be a dancer from the time I was a little girl. It's all I could think about. It's where I found peace and sanity in my hectic and insane world. Some days when my mother was home she, would turn on the stereo and just start dancing with me in the living room of our two-bedroom apartment. My mother wanted to be a dancer, but being a very young single mother of three made it impossible for her. Dancing was the only time I ever saw her truly happy. It made me want the same happiness.

"Why don't we go talk to your father about this?" I ask.

Andrea shakes her head. "He won't listen. Me and my mom tried to talk to him about it. He says it's fine as a hobby but I need to have a real job and be like Sean and open my own business."

"You can have your own business in dance. You are your own business. And you're as passionate about dance as I am so I'm sure you'd be successful."

Andrea takes a long deep breath. "Maybe I'll talk to him about it again. I just can't see myself doing anything other than dance."

I stand and walk to Andrea. "Don't say maybe, do it. I'll come with you."

I hold my hand out for Andrea to take. She looks at me for a while unsure of what to do. I smile at her to let her know it's OK. She reluctantly puts her hand in mine. As I lead Andrea up the stairs, my heart starts to beat. I don't want to get on Mr. Winters' bad side, yet at the same time I can't stand to see Andrea give up her dream because he can't see her passion. We get to the second floor and walk right past Toni who's standing at the stove frying chicken.

"Dinner's ready, girls." Toni says.

"We'll be there in a minute." I tell her.

We walk to the office door which I found out earlier was Sean's old bedroom. Andrea tries to walk away but my firm grip on her hand forces her to stay. I can tell she's having second thoughts. To be honest, so am I. We both just stand at the door, neither one of us wanting to knock.

"What are you girls doing?" Toni asks from the kitchen.

I look back at her and smile. "About to become an adult."

I nudge Andrea. She looks at me, then rolls her eyes. She takes a deep breath, then lightly knocks on the door.

"Come in."

Andrea opens the door and she and I walk in. Mr. Winters looks at us and it looks as if he's scared at the ambush. He knows something is up and my guess is he thinks we're going to ask for something he doesn't want to give. I sit in one of the chairs in front of his desk while Andrea continues to stand. He takes his glasses off and sits back in his chair a little annoyed at the interruption. It looks as if he's working on his sermon for Sunday's anniversary service.

"How much?" Mr. Winters asks before Andrea can say anything.

Andrea shakes her head. "I don't want money, Daddy. I need to talk to you."

Mr. Winters changes his demeanor to be more attentive. His baby seems like she has something on her mind and he wants to let her know he's listening. "What's wrong?"

"I decided that I'm going to major in dance and not business."

Mr. Winters looks at me with irritation. "You put her up to this?"

I shrug my shoulders. "Yes and no...."

He cuts me off. "So is that what you girls do? It's bad enough you dance around in your underwear for the world to see but you have to recruit young naïve girls to do it as well? No daughter of mine is going to become eye candy for a bunch of horny, perverted men."

"Stop it, Daddy. That's mean."

I have to admit I'm a little offended and ticked off. How dare he make an assumption like that? I have never danced in my underwear. Photographed, yes. But I have never danced around in my underwear for no one except Sean. I feel my anger rising but I keep a calm cool demeanor about myself. "Have you ever seen my work? Or, are you just going off what you've heard?"

"Young lady, I don't need to see your work. I've seen it all before you were even born. Models are nothing more than little sex pots that make men fantasize about them."

"So, you've never fantasized about your wife?" I ask deliberately trying to get under his skin. Men hate when you turn the tables on them.

"What kind of question is that? Are you trying to get on my bad side?"

I stand. It's time to turn up the heat on him. "All I'm saying is that beautiful women are fantasized about no matter what they do. Dancing and modeling are all art. It's an expression of art and Andrea is passionate about dancing."

Now he stands. It almost seems that if he can't prove his point, he's going to try and intimidate me by becoming bigger than me. " I'm not going to talk about this anymore. Andrea you are going to major in business because that's stable."

Andrea tries to stand up to her father. "What if I go to business school and end up opening my own dance studio?"

Mr. Winters is stuck speechless. He looks at me again. "You've only been here a day and already you've got my daughter thinking she wants to do something she doesn't want to do. Stop filling her head with thoughts that dancing is more than shaking your ass in front of people."

186

"Ronald!" Toni screams from the doorway.

We all look at Toni standing in the doorway with hands on hips.

Andrea turns back to her father. "Daddy, please listen. I want to dance as bad as Sean wants to take pictures."

"Dancing isn't the way to get it, Baby. Alexis sells an image of sex, that's all. That's not for you."

Andrea tears up and walks out of the office.

"Ronald, I'm not going to have you be disrespectful to Alexis. She is going to marry Sean. She's a part of this family now and you will treat her as such."

Mr. Winters sits back in his chair. "She can be a part of this family. Doesn't mean I have to like what she does for a living or allow her to convince my daughter to make poor decisions."

Instead of saying anything that might cause further arguing, I decide to walk out as well. As I walk to the kitchen I hear Toni scolding Mr. Winters. I start to think maybe Sean was right about his father. I'm regretting my decision to cancel our hotel reservations. If I hadn't, I may be with Sean right now making love instead of him being off somewhere else right now.

I sit at the kitchen table and look at my engagement ring. The princess cut two and one half carat diamond ring is everything I could ever want. But right now I'm not very happy. I'm not stupid. I know where Sean is. I'm well aware the argument we had in the car did nothing but push him away. It probably made him think about all the good times he had with Summer where there was no arguing. I should have never told Sean to talk to her to see where their feelings were. I have a feeling that if Sean talks to Summer it will be the end of our relationship. I finally found a good man and I pushed him into another woman's arms and the thought of Sean sleeping with Summer right now keeps popping into my head.

Chapter 13

Sean

Summer texted me her address while I was on my way to her place. I stop by Jack'n'the Box on Telegraph Avenue and grab something to eat. I am starving and it also gives Summer time to get home and clean up a little. I'm pretty sure that's why she told me to meet her in a half-hour when it only takes about five minutes to get to her place from my parents. I can just picture it. She's running through the place picking up clothes and underwear. She's trying to put dishes in the dishwasher. She's wiping down her table and counter. I bet she's even putting all of her magazines in order.

As I sit and eat my spicy chicken sandwich and curly fries, I think back to how Summer always wanted everything perfect. Even her first time, even though it wasn't planned for us to lose our virginity to each other, it still came out perfect for both of us.

I remember it like my favorite song. It was prom night at the Marriot in downtown Oakland. I'd brought a date, a girl I'd gone out with a few times. Her name was Sonia White. She was cute and a virgin like me. I was sure the night was going to end with us in bed. I bought about six condoms just in case I broke the first few seeing as I had never put one on before.

Summer had come with her boyfriend of the last two years, Chris, aka Mr. Basketball, who was actually getting recruited by U. C L. A, Duke, North Carolina and Syracuse. Eric would joke with him saying he wasn't good enough for any of those schools. He and Summer had been together for such a long time that I thought for sure that they had started having sex. But that wasn't the case; at least the two of them weren't having sex together. Chris was having sex with a bunch of girls I knew about. Me, Eric and Natalie all tried to tell Summer but she was in love and couldn't hear us.

I remember Sonia was getting
annoyed with me because I spent
the whole night taking pictures for
the yearbook and she wanted to
dance. I couldn't help it though.
Pictures to me are memories
captured forever. It's nice to have
good memories, especially when
you've had some bad things happen
in your life.

I was having a good time
snapping photos when I aimed my
lens at Summer and Chris in the
corner of the room. They were
arguing and it looked like it was
getting heated. I started to go over
and break it, up but my mother
always told me to never get involved
with a couple's argument. You may
think you're coming to the woman's
rescue but she'll get pissed at you
for jumping in her and her man's
business. All of a sudden, I saw
Summer mouth the words "it's
over", then walk out of the room,
nearly in tears. Chris looked upset
for a second until another girl
walked up to him and began to flirt.
Summer was quickly a distant
memory to him.

I look to the dance floor and
see Sonia had found another guy to
dance with so I didn't feel bad when

I went after Summer. I found her standing by the elevators patting her eyes with a tissue. I jog to her and get on the elevator just before the doors close. She's quiet and I'm not sure what to say so I do what I do best and take a picture of her.

"Sean, that's not funny." She says trying to fight back more tears.

"What's wrong, Summer?"

We reach a floor, I don't remember which, but she gets off and I follow her. We walk down a few rooms and Summer stops. She pulls out her key card from her purse and opens the door. She looks at me for a few seconds then walks in. A little unsure, I follow Summer into the room. She throws her purse on the nightstand and plops down on the bed. I stand at the foot of the bed and take another picture.

"Sean, I'm going to break that camera if you take another picture." She says, obviously annoyed.

"You want to be alone?" I ask. I don't want to get on her bad side. I was just concerned about her. I saw what happened between her and Chris. It looked as if she needed a friend. Natalie and Eric were already gone by that time so I guess I was it.

"If I wanted to be alone, I wouldn't have let you follow me up here or come into the room." She says, taking a deep breath.

I know what's on her mind. Everybody in the school had been talking about Chris getting offered to play for U. C L. A and he was going to accept. If she thought his cheating was bad now, just wait until he's playing college ball.

"You guys were right." She says. "I knew he was cheating but I just thought it was because I wasn't giving him any. How did he expect for me to give him my virginity if he was always with another girl?"

That was news to me. I just assumed that Summer and Chris had started sleeping with each other just because they had been together almost two years. I guess I was wrong. So I'm not the only virgin in our group of friends. Eric had started as soon as he got his car at sixteen. Natalie had confided in me that she started having sex with her boyfriend earlier in the year. This made Summer even more beautiful to me because she didn't just give herself to anyone. She had respect for herself and I respected that.

"I thought for sure if I told him I would sleep with him tonight he would stop cheating. He told me I would always be his main girl and that any other girl would just be sex."

Summer looks at me with those big brown eyes filling with tears that she won't let fall. I want to hold her and comfort her. I want to make her smile again. I want to go back downstairs and beat Chris all the way up and down Broadway.

"I broke up with him. This time for good."

Summer and Chris always had an up and down relationship. They broke up at least once a month after he got caught cheating again. He'd buy her flowers and candy or dedicate a winning game to her and all would be forgiven. I guess she always thought he would change.

"I really thought tonight would be the night I lost my virginity." She says. She went on to tell me about how she saved up for months in order to afford the room. She even paid Natalie to make the dress she was wearing. Natalie usually didn't charge us. She also tells me how she bought condoms and lingerie for the evening. She was so excited about tonight, she let his flirting with other girls roll off of her back. But she said she caught him outside kissing another girl tonight and that was the last straw. She gave up trying to make him be someone he wasn't.

I set my camera down on the dresser in front of the bed. I take a seat next to Summer and give her a hug. I hold her firm as she squeezes tight. I rub her back for extra comfort. Her skin felt soft and smooth. I release the hug and wipe the tears from her eyes.

"Are you still a virgin, Sean?" She asks.

The question caught me off guard. I wanted to tell her no and make myself seem like a bit of a player. I got a little nervous. The last time Summer asked me if I had ever done anything she kissed me. I started to think the same thing was going to happen and we were going to have sex. Those thoughts went to both heads and she noticed.

"You are aren't you?" She asks with a smile.

I start to stand but I decide against it. I figured it was best to answer while seated. "I had the same plan as you. But I doubt Sonia is going to be interested seeing as I haven't danced with her once tonight and I just left her to come see about you."

"Who would you rather sleep with, Sonia or me?" Summer asks.

I'm not sure if she's joking or being serious. Either way it wasn't a hard question to answer. Summer has been the girl next door since she moved next door. I've always had fantasies about sexing her more than any other woman I've come across. I remember she used to let me suck on her tits a few years back, but it never went any further than that, though I wanted it to. Sonia, on the other hand, was just a girl taking up time as far I was concerned. I wasn't in love with her; I barely liked her. She was just a girl who said yes when I asked her out on a date.

Summer puts her hand between my legs. "I guess that's my answer," she says as she leans in and kisses me.

"Summer, what are you doing? I thought we agreed to just be friends," I tell her not wanting to cause any issues in our friendship, but also not wanting her to stop.

Summer sits back and looks at me. "You are my friend and that's why I want to lose my virginity to you and no one else."

I lean in this time and kiss her. I glide my tongue into her mouth and play with hers. She wraps her hand around neck and pulls me to her. She leans back on the bed and I climb on top of her and rest in between her legs. I can't believe this is happening and with Summer. I was actually about to have sex with the girl of my dreams. I tried to get my mind off of it because I felt myself about explode. Eric told me that you should start thinking about other things so you don't give out too fast.

Summer pulled her dress down and her yellow skin revealed her soft breasts. They had grown since the last time I had seen them. I begin to suck the right, then the left, then back and forth for a few minutes as she goes crazy. I then look in her eyes and she bites her lip. She wanted me just as much as I wanted her.

I kiss her again as she takes off my tuxedo jacket. We both sit up

197

on our knees as I get the jacket off.
She quickly unbuttons my shirt as I
unbuckle my pants. She kisses my
chest then my neck, which almost
brings me to climax again. I know
something escaped before I could
stop it. After a few seconds, I'm in
nothing but my boxers as I pull her
dress off slowly. I can tell she's still
self-conscious about her body. She
shouldn't have been, it was perfect.
She was thick in all the right places
and slim everywhere else.

She grabs her purse and pulls
out a condom and hands it to me. I
get nervous because I had never put
a condom on before, so I started
reading the instructions on the back
of the package. Summer giggles at
me.

"You don't remember sex class
when they showed us how to put the
condom on the banana?"

I actually think I was home
sick that day, but I didn't want to
tell her that. She sees me struggling
and pulls my boxers down, takes
the condom out of the package and
slides it on me. She smiles and
looks in my eyes the whole time.
Once it's on, she lies back on the
bed. I pull down her sexy red
lingerie from Victoria's Secret. I

climbed back between her legs and pinch myself to see if this is really happening. It is. Summer helps me to find her secret place. I slowly slide myself in and out until both of us are comfortable with the fit. Summer puts her hands on my back as I move inside of her. We both moan and groan for what seems like forever. Finally, I couldn't hold it anymore and I release inside of her and collapse on top of her. She hugs me and kisses my forehead.

"You're no longer a virgin, Honey," she says as she kisses me again.

"Neither are you," I tell her as I slowly pull myself out of her magical world and lay next to her.

She lays her head on my chest.

"Are you okay?" I ask her, wondering if it was good for her. Looking at the clock, it only lasted about three minutes.

"I'm glad it was you," she says.

We kiss again, passionately, like lovers, which we now were.

"How do you feel?" She asks.

I look at her and smile. "I feel like I want to do it again."

She laughs at me. "I got a box full of condoms and the room for the night."

And that was our first time together. Although we never said we were boyfriend and girlfriend, we continued to have sex until we went off to college. Sonia didn't talk to me after that night. I guess I hurt her. And Chris made it to U. C. L. A. After college he got drafted to the Clippers and is now in three different custody disputes.

I pull into a guest parking space at Summer's condo, park and walk up a flight of stairs to get to her place. I pause for a moment before ringing the doorbell. I'm wondering if this is the right decision or am I walking into what could be the worst mistake of my life. On the one hand, I will finally know where Summer and I stand. On the other hand, I could be ruining my chances with a good woman already wearing my ring. If I choose not to talk to Summer, then I'll always wonder what if.

I take a deep breath and ring the doorbell. I start to walk away when I hear Summer call out, "Just a minute." She sounds so sweet and sexy at the same time. I know

she's double-checking her place to
make sure nothing is out of place.
Everything always has to be perfect
for her. For as long as I can
remember, she has always been
such a perfectionist.

A few seconds pass and finally I
hear the door unlock and open.
Summer stands in the doorway in a
pair of pink sweats and a black wife
beater. Her hair is pulled back in a
ponytail. All the make-up she wore
earlier has been washed off and she
only wears some Mac lip-gloss. I
don't know what she's trying to get
across with her outfit. When I saw
her this afternoon, she had the tight
grey dress and black boots and her
hair hung straight just above her
shoulders. She looked sexy then,
but now she looks beautiful.

I have to admit that I like when
a woman dresses up and looks sexy,
but I love when a woman is just laid
back and comfortable. Any woman
can look better with make-up but a
beautiful woman doesn't need it.

Summer smiles at me and I
smile back. She reaches up and
hugs me and gives me a kiss on the
cheek. She then invites me into her
condo. I look around as she closes
the door. We stand in her living

room, which has a nice love seat against one wall and a flat screen TV against the opposite wall. A glass coffee table sits in the middle of the room and two expensive looking grey chairs sit on each side of the love seat. Off to the right she has a nice size kitchen with orange pastel cabinets and stainless steel appliances. In the dinning room sits a glass table with four orange chairs.

"You want to sit?" She asks as she walks to her love seat.

I reluctantly walk over and sit next to her. The longer I sit next to her, the more I become intoxicated with her scent. The perfume she is wearing is driving me crazy. It makes me want to kiss her neck and taste her sweetness. We sit for a moment in awkward silence, not knowing what to say to each other.

"Why did you walk away from me earlier?" I ask her.

"Why didn't you tell me you were engaged?" She fires back.

I don't know how to answer because I honestly don't know the answer. When Summer called me last night, I could have told her then, but I didn't. I could have told her while we were talking earlier,

but I didn't. Maybe I really wanted
to know what she wanted to talk to
me about before dropping the
bombshell. If she told me she
wanted me back, then I would have
no reason to tell her because I
would have broken it off with Alexis.
Or would I have?

"Look, you wanted to tell me
something last night. What was it?"
I ask trying to avoid answering her
question.

"I wanted to talk about us," she
says as she puts her hand on my
leg.

I feel my temperature among
other things rising. Her touch could
bring me to climax but I hold strong,
trying to be in control of this
situation. If I lose control, I'll regret
it, maybe.

"Summer, there hasn't been an
us for over two years," I tell her.

"Are you really serious about
getting married?"

"Why?" I'm curious, wondering
if she is jealous.

"You've never been serious with
a woman in your life, Honey. Except
for me. I find it hard to believe you
want to get married."

I look deep into Summer's eyes
and say, "Maybe you should have

been serious with me and you just might be the one who is getting married."

Summer drops her jaw and sits back. "How can you say that? I was always serious with you. You were my first everything."

"But never your only."

I got her with that. Out of all the times we were together over the years, she always had another guy or two she could go out with in case she got bored with me.

"You were my only. The only one I truly loved," she tells me as she gets close again.

"Then why did you always brake it off with me when another guy came around?"

She puts her hand on the side of my face. "Because I was stupid and I guess I thought you would always be there. I love you, Sean. Then and now."

Summer and I stare into each other's eyes for a second. I start to look at her soft pink lips. I start to lean in for a kiss. She closes her eyes giving me permission to go for it. I get so close I can taste her breath. Then my phone rings. The volume of my ring tone startles both of us. Summer opens her eyes and sits back. I lean back and reach into the back pocket of my jeans and pull out my IPhone. It's Alexis.

"You're not really going to answer that are you?" Summer asks with attitude.

I can't ignore Alexis, that would just be wrong. I answer the call. "Hey, Lexis."

"Where did you go?" She asks with a little irritation and concern mixed in with some hurt.

"I had to clear my head for a second, so I went for a drive."

"Look I'm sorry, Baby. I'm letting my insecurities get the best of me. I know you wouldn't do anything to hurt me. I love you."

That is weird, two women saying they love me within two minutes. I should be the happiest man in the world. Two beautiful, intelligent, independent women are really in love with me. I look at Summer who is irritated, rolling her eyes because she wants me right now. I have Alexis on the phone who wants me to come back to her right now. What's a brotha to do?

"I'll be back in a minute, Lexis. Okay. I love you too."

I hang-up the phone, making sure it's hung up and locked and put it back into my pocket. I take a deep breath and look at Summer.

"So, I guess you're going?" Summer asks already knowing the answer.

I nod my head.

"You don't want to finish what we started?"

I nod my head again. "I do, but I can't. I can't leave this one for you just to have to you break-up with me when another man comes around that you like."

I kiss Summer on the cheek and stand and head for the door. Summer stands and stops me at the door.

"I'm sorry for hurting you, but the two of us belong together. It's taken me a long time to figure that out but I did. We're a perfect fit and I want you as mine for always. I've made you break-up with a bunch of women for me but I promise you that if you break-up with Alexis, she would be last one."

"I'm sure you believe that."

I kiss Summer on the forehead and walk out the door.

Chapter 14

Summer

"What the hell just happened?"
I was ready to prove to Sean that I loved him by giving him the best sex he ever had. How dare he walk out on me? I walk to my freezer and pull out a bottle of Ciroc Vodka. Regular wine is not going to relax me tonight. I get some cranberry juice out of the refrigerator and a small glass out of the glass cabinet just above the dishwasher. I pour in the cranberry juice before the Ciroc and mix it with my finger. I taste my finger and am satisfied.

I walk to my bedroom only to be disappointed. I got home quick. I didn't need to straighten up because my house is always neat. I was so excited that Sean was coming over and wanted to make sure it was special. I lit four lavender scented candles in each corner of the room. I had slow jams playing low. The bed is made perfect, with the comforter folded to the foot of the bed, making it easier to get in then cover up. I had some Africa's Best oil on the night stand along with a bottle of Moscato and two wine glasses. I was definitely going to give Sean the night of his life. Damn Alexis had to mess it all up by calling my man.

"He doesn't know what he missed." I say as I blow the candles out and turn the music off.

Just looking at the room upsets me so I go back to the living room, turn the TV on and try to find something halfway decent to watch on a Friday night. There's a rerun of The Real House Wives of Atlanta on so I decide to watch it. I take a sip of my cranberry and vodka and another and another and another. I normally save my Ciroc for when Natalie or some co-workers come over for girls night. Usually, I just have a glass of wine to relax in the evening. But tonight I needed something to try and make me forget that I was lonely. The only problem is the vodka is making me feel the need for some loving. And

now I'm mad because I was so close
to getting some tonight.

I can't figure out whether I'm
angry or hurt or both. I know I'm
pissed. I put all that work into
making the bedroom look special
and Sean didn't even get to see it.
We were just about to kiss before
Alexis called and pulled him away.
Out of all the other times Alexis
could have come to town to visit,
she chooses this time. The time
when I should have Sean all to
myself. That's my fault though.
Over the past two years, every time
Sean came to visit I made it a point
to miss him. I was so confused
because I wanted to see him each
time he was in town, but it just
didn't seem right. The last two
times we talked he seemed cold and
distant. I knew he was serious with
Alexis so I passed the time trying to
get serious with my ex-fiancée,
Jackson.

Thinking about Jackson only
makes me feel more lonely. Maybe I
should call him for a quickie since I
had everything ready for a sex fest
and no one to share it with. But that
wouldn't be a good idea because
Jackson would think it was a sign
that we were getting back together.

And I have always vowed never to go backwards, except for Sean. But that's not going backwards because Sean has always been there. Sean has been my steady man since we were twelve and no one can come between that.

When a commercial hits, I go to the kitchen to refill my glass. I put the Ciroc back in the freezer hoping it will keep me from coming back for a third glass. I take a sip of my newly refreshed glass and walk back to my love seat just as my cell phone begins to ring. A piece of me is hoping it's Sean telling me he's changed his mind and is coming back to help me release this sexual tension I have built up inside of me. When I pick up the phone and see the caller ID, I sigh, and answer my best friend's call.

"Hey, Nat." I was not in the mood to talk to anyone, especially Natalie who pissed me off earlier.

"Summer, I just wanted to apologize for earlier. I may have overstepped my boundaries telling what you should do with your heart and all."

"You're damn right you overstepped your boundaries!" I guess the vodka and cranberry gave me a boost of courage. Plus Natalie was on the phone and not in front of me so I don't have to worry about her slapping the hell out of me.

"Look, girl, I'm apologizing. Do you accept it or not?"

I pause for a minute trying to hold on to my anger but I can't. I've never been able to stay mad at Natalie for long. We've been best friends for fifteen years. Natalie saved me several times from getting beat up in high school when my mouth wrote a check that my ass couldn't cash. I love Natalie like a sister and I know she's only looking out for me, even if it seems she's more on Alexis' side right now.

"I forgive you, Nat."

"Good," Natalie says. "Now have you decided what you're going to do because I don't want any drama at my grand opening tomorrow?"

I tell Natalie everything. I tell her how I have done a lot of thinking and soul searching and realize that Sean is the one. I was too busy trying to explore that I pushed my one true love away. I tell her I'm scared that I may have lost Sean forever. I go into detail about my evening plans with Sean and how I had the bedroom set up for lovemaking and how right when we were about to kiss Alexis called and got Sean to leave before we had a chance to do anything. I tell her how Sean didn't hesitate to leave and how he told me that he wasn't sure if I truly wanted to be with him and only him.

"If he would have just let me put it on him, it would have worked and we would be in the middle of making love right now."

"It didn't work because you went about it wrong." Natalie finally has a chance to speak.

'What are you talking about?"

"You went into this expecting sex and not having a plan for the future. You need to tell Sean how you see your future with him."

I finish my second glass before speaking. "All a man needs to know is that the woman he's with is going to give him the ass when and how he wants it."

Natalie giggles. "See, that's why it was so easy for Sean to get up and leave yo ass sitting there lonely. He knows what the future holds for him and Alexis. All he could see with you is a quick lay."

I take offense to Natalie's statement. "I have never been a quick lay to anybody. I'm not a ho."

"Then tell me, Summer, why, when Sean has only been in town a few hours, did you have your bedroom set up for sex? What were you going to do afterwards?"

I can't answer Natalie's question because I really hadn't thought about the afterwards part. All I know is that I wanted to feel Sean inside of me again and make him forget about Alexis. But what would I have done after? Sean lives in LA and I live in Oakland. My pediatric practice is here and Sean's photography studio is in L. A. How would we make that work? Natalie is right. I don't have a plan for our future. I just know that my future wouldn't be right if Sean wasn't in it.

"That's exactly what I've been trying to get you see," Natalie says when I don't answer. "I can hear it in your voice that you're in love with Sean but you can't expect him to leave Alexis just because you throw sex in his face. You need to make him realize it wouldn't be the same old thing as before where you would

213

drop him when another man comes around."

"I hear you, Nat. I hear you."

"Good. Now get some rest so you can be ready for tomorrow." Natalie says.

"Alright, girl. I'll talk to you later."

I hang up the phone trying to figure out my next move. I need to find a way to convince Sean that I will never leave him for another man again. How do I get him to see that he's the only man for me and has always been the only man for me? I have to come up with a better plan than just sex. I have to think about our future. The crazy thing is whenever I have thought about my future; Sean has always been in it, right beside me. Sean has always been the person I have felt most comfortable and safe with. That's why I ventured out so much. I was young and immature and being safe and secure wasn't so appealing. I needed a little bit of danger and drama to make me feel alive. But now I'm pushing thirty and being safe and secure is all I want. Sean is all I want.

214

Chapter 15

Sean

Driving back to my parents' place, I just can't stop thinking about what just transpired. I can't believe I just walked away from some free sex. It was right there for me to take it and I just walked away. Granted, my decision came from me not wanting to disappoint Alexis but still, I walked away from my first love, the girl of my dreams. Summer was ready and willing to give it to me and I walked away. What is wrong with me? I came up here to find out if Summer and I still had a connection and when I find out she still wants me, I walk away. I need to slap myself for not taking it when it was offered to me. Now I probably will never get the chance again. Although, knowing Summer, she always gets what she wants. So if she wants me bad enough, she'll try again before the weekend is over.

Trying to get my mind of off my poor decision, I put my Bluetooth in my ear and dial Melanie's number. I want to make sure my studio is still in tact and all went well with the shoot. I don't like letting people use my studio without me there, but I trust Melanie to keep things in order.

"Hey, Sean," Melanie answers, sounding a little winded.

"You okay, Melanie?"

"Yeah, just trying to clean up the studio, after the wild party we just had here."

"What!" I scream into the phone. "What party?"

I know they better not have thrown a party in my studio. I will fire both her and Miles. If they messed up my equipment, they are going to wish they were in another country. I don't play with my studio.

"Ease-up, Sean, I'm just joking," Melanie says with a giggle.

I don't find it funny, but I change my tone. "So everything went alright then?"

"What you thought? It wasn't?"

She tells me all about the photo shoot. She tells me that Miles is actually a good photographer and his wife was beautiful and should be a model. She goes on to explain that Miles has some real creative ways of shooting and that I should think about hiring him as photographer and get another assistant.

"He's that good?" I ask.

"He may be better than you," she jokes.

"I'll look at his work when I get back. Not promising anything, but it may drum up more business having a third photographer. Lord knows I've been bringing in the business for us."

Melanie sucks her teeth before speaking. "Please! With all the artists Paul refers to the studio, I should be a partner in the business. Can you say fifty/fifty?"

"Whatever." I change the subject. "I ran into Summer up here."

Melanie takes a deep breath. She knows all about Summer. I talked about her all the time. Melanie never really put her opinion out there except once. She told me that Summer had me whipped. I told her I wasn't whipped, I was in love. But thinking back, maybe I was, maybe I still am.

"Don't tell me all your old feelings resurfaced and now you don't know what do?"

"You know me too well." I tell her.

"Does Alexis know about Summer?"

I tell her I've laid it all out for Alexis a long time ago. I told her that Alexis never seemed too worried about Summer until we got to Oakland. I even tell her about the encounter I just had with Summer and how I walked away. She quietly listens to me tell her the whole story as I park in front of my parents' house and turn off the engine.

"I'm going to tell you like this, Sean, you're a good man and Alexis is a good woman and from what you told me, Summer is a good woman. What you need to do is to start thinking with your head, and not the one between your legs. The one between your legs will always get you into trouble but the one on your shoulders will give you clear direction."

She makes perfect sense. I mean the head between my legs only wants to go in one direction and that's the sweet spot. The one on my shoulders led me back to Alexis.

I guess that's it. Alexis is the one I want to be with.

"I understand, Melanie, thanks."

"No, problem. See you Tuesday."

We hang up and I take the Bluetooth out of my ear. I know Alexis is the one for me and that she is the woman I am going to marry. I know this because I came back to her even when I could have had Summer tonight. I feel more confident in my decision now. I get out of the car and put on the alarm. I walk up the red stairs and ring the doorbell. Andrea opens the door a few seconds and a few locks later.

"Hey, Sean, your fiancée is cool. You better not mess this up."

I walk into the house and see Alexis and my mother sitting at the kitchen table. Alexis looks at me and smiles. She stands and walks over to the oven where a plate of fried chicken, greens and corn bread are being heated. Alexis takes an oven mitt from the side of the stove and pulls the plate out.

"We saved you a plate, Baby," Alexis says as she places the plate on top of the stove and closes the oven door.

"Where the heck have you been, Sean?" My mother says still sitting but glaring at me.

"I just went for a drive," I tell her

"You left Alexis here by herself. That's no way to treat the girl you're about marry, especially if this is the first time she's meeting your family."

I walk to Alexis and kiss her and hug her tight. "I know, I'm sorry."

"Me and Andrea had to keep her company. I'm sure she's tired of teaching dance moves and hearing my voice."

Alexis breaks the hug and walks to my mother and hugs her shoulders. "I could never get tired of hearing your voice. And I was glad to teach Andrea that dance step."

Andrea walks to the table and sits. "You made it look so easy."

Alexis sits as well. "It just takes practice. I've been praise dancing since I was a little girl."

"Thanks anyway, Sis."

Andrea is already calling Alexis Sis. I guess we're becoming a little family. I grab my plate of food and sit down in what is usually my father's chair, across from my

mother and in the middle of Alexis
and Andrea. I tear into the first
piece of chicken and fall in love with
my mother's cooking all over again.
Even though I had a meal at
Jack'n'the Box not too long ago, I
made sure not to eat too much
because I knew I wasn't going to get
away with not eating my mother's
home cooking.

As I eat, Alexis, my mother and
Andrea continue to talk like they're
old friends. My mother tells stories
about me getting in trouble as a kid
and how I would hide under my bed
so I wouldn't get a whooping. It
always failed though. I always got it
in the end. Andrea tells stories
about how I made her do everything
for me like she was my maid. I
made her clean my room and the
bathroom, even though we shared it.

I finish eating, stuffed to the
top and unable to move. I feel like
unbuckling my belt to release some
of the pressure. I'm ready to go
downstairs and go to sleep. Alexis
yawns, signaling she's tired too. It's
not that late, only about seven-
thirty. I think the long drive wore
us out as well. Not to mention we
didn't get much sleep last night
because we were celebrating our

engagement into the wee hours of the morning.

"So, have you guys set a date yet?" Andrea is so excited about me getting married. She seems more excited than Alexis.

Before I can answer, I hear the door to my old room open up and my father calls out. "Sean, can you come in here for a minute?"

I wanted to yell out "Hell no," but I decided against it. Alexis pats me on my hand trying to get me to get up and go talk with The Good Reverend Winters. I take a napkin and wipe my hands and mouth then reluctantly get up and walk across the kitchen to my father's office. I step in and close the door behind me.

The Good Reverend Winters sits at his desk going over notes. He looks a lot older than what I remember. He has more grey hair than black and he's starting to move slower. At this moment I almost feel a little sorry for him. I'm trying to search my heart for forgiveness for what he did but I can't find it. It's a hard thing for a kid to handle when his father disappoints him. My father disappointed me, and he has tried for years to make it up me but it hasn't been enough.

"Sit down, Son." He gestures for me to sit down in one of the chairs near his desk.

I sit, trying to figure out what he called me in the office for. I know I'm too old to be in trouble for something like getting a D on my report card. And I did get a few of those.

"Sean, I know you don't think I meant it when I said I'm sorry earlier, but I wanted you to know that I am. I am truly sorry for letting you down, Son."

"I just don't understand why you did it. You're supposed to be a Christian leader and you failed."

The Good Reverend Winters breaks down the entire story to me. He says he's not making any excuses. What he did was wrong and it was a moment of weakness. He tells how he's been faced with the temptation of many beautiful women in the church wanting to sleep with him. He told me how Andrea's mother was crying and needed comforting and the comforting led to them becoming intimate with each other. Afterwards, they both agreed it was a mistake and Tricia decided to find another church home.

Now my father could have not said anything and just let the transgression go. My mother would have never known, but he couldn't live with himself if he didn't tell her. He said he came home that night and told my mother the whole story. He said my mother was livid and was ready to head to divorce court the very next morning. My father slept downstairs that night and several nights after that. It took months before my mother decided to give him another chance and put the incident behind them.

Several months later, my father got a call from Tricia saying she was pregnant but didn't want anything from him. The only thing she wanted was to put his name on the birth certificate in case anything happened. It took another several months before my mother could forgive my father again, but she did.

Then came news Tricia was killed during a car accident on the way home from work to get Andrea. Andrea was only four months old. My father got the call and since he was on the birth certificate, he was the legal guardian. He told me my mother made him go get Andrea but that she wasn't going to help him raise her. My father brought Andrea home and we all fell in love with her. My mother stayed true to her word for only a couple of weeks, but she couldn't help wanting to take care of Andrea too. After all, it wasn't Andrea's fault her parents made a big mistake.

By the end of the story, The Good Reverend Winters was near tears. I too had watery eyes, but neither of us were going to cry. I have to admit after hearing the whole story, I wasn't as mad at my father. He did take responsibility for his actions. I stood up from my chair and shook his hand. The first time I had got this close to my father in years was right now. He stands and hugs me and apologizes again. I hug him back still trying to fight tears.

I break the hug. "It's not going to happen over night but I'll work on forgiveness." I tell him.

"I'll take that, Son."

I look at the clock on his desk and see that over an hour has passed with his story. I walk out of the office and close the door behind me. The kitchen light is off and no one is to be found. I peek out the kitchen window and see Andrea's car is gone. She probably went out with some friends. It is Friday night. I walk to my parents room and hear a TV going so I figured my mother was in bed. I walk to the door that leads downstairs and open it. I close it behind me and lock it as I walk down the stairs.

Alexis sits on the bed watching the old TV that's off to the side of the dresser. She looks at me and smiles. I smile back seeing as she's only in her panties and bra and they are a matching purple set. It looks like she just got out of the shower. Her hair is wet and curly, and her body glows from baby oil and moisture. I begin to get excited looking at the woman I'm going to marry.

She breaks my train of thought. "Andrea asked a good question tonight. I hadn't thought about setting a date for the wedding yet. What do you think?"

"I think you should ask me that question when you're not half naked." I sit on the bed next to Alexis and kiss her neck.

She gently pushes me away.
"I'm being serious Sean. I want to
know what you think."

I look at Alexis and say,
"Septunuary."

She laughs and lightly slaps me
on my chest. I kiss her softly. I
glide my tongue in her mouth and
play with hers.

"Promise me you'll think of a
date," she says with her hands
around my neck in between kisses.

"I promise."

We get back to kissing. I lean
her back on to the bed and climb on
top of her in between her legs.

"I thought you said the walls
are thin here. I don't want your
mother and the preacher to here
us." Alexis has a not so worried
look on her face.

"We'll be fine, just internalize."

She giggles, then kisses me. I
kiss her from her head, to her neck,
to her breast, all the while making
her hot. She breathes deep as I get
to her breast. I pull the bra to the
side and grab a tit and put as much
in mouth as would fit. I suck hard
on the nipple which makes her go
crazy. I rub her through her panties
and she gets juicy and I stand at
attention.

I pull her panties down, then kiss one leg, then the other, then back and forth until I reach heaven on earth. I begin to kiss her lips. My tongue finds her pearl and I go at it like my favorite dessert, savoring every bite. Alexis takes some of the pillows and puts them over her face to muffle her moans. It doesn't take long for me to make her give me a brainstorm. Her body shakes and shivers as she tries to hold the pillow over her face and keep from screaming in excitement.

I smile and wipe the juices off of my chin. I smile at her as she finally takes the pillow from her face out of breath. She looks at me as if she wants me inside her more than ever. I'm pleased with how I've made her feel. Nothing pleases me more during sex than making my woman climax. She motions with her finger for me to finish the job. I pull down my jeans and underwear and climb on top of her. I enter her innermost walls slowly and gently because I know she's still sensitive. When I'm all the way in she puts her arms around my back and I begin to please her. Pleasing her pleases me.

"Take your shirt off, I want my nails in your back." She says in between moans.

I get up on my knees, still inside, and with one arm pull off my button down shirt and under shirt and throw them to the side. I get back to business as Alexis digs her nails into my back. As I stroke, I kiss her neck. I can feel her about to get loud so I kiss her lips and make her bite my bottom lip to keep her quiet. I close my eyes and think about how good this is.

When I open my eyes I'm shocked to see Summer's face where Alexis' face should be. I start to pull out but decided against it. I make my strokes longer and harder not knowing if I'm trying to erase the image of Summer or if I'm trying harder to please the image of Summer. Whatever it is, I'm starting to make her get louder and louder and before I know it I'm exploding inside of her. My body weak, I fall on top of her as she kisses my neck.

"I love you, Baby." Alexis' voice comes out.

I lift myself up and see Alexis is the one lying with me. I'm relieved and disappointed at the same time.

Relieved because I thought I was trippin' and may have been going crazy. Disappointed because now I'm thinking maybe I should have slept with Summer one last time to get her out of my system. Unless I do it, I'm always going to think what if. Alexis is the woman I want to marry, but Summer is the one that keeps me from giving myself fully to her.

"I'm going to take a shower." I tell Alexis.

"I'm going to sleep. I hope your parents didn't hear us."

I slowly pull out, get up and walk to the bathroom and get in the shower. The warm water fells good, relaxing. Too many thoughts are running through my head. Every time I try to push Summer out of my head, she pops back in. I can't seem to move past her. I want her more than I knew. There is something about Summer that makes me forget everything and everyone else. For the past two years she was the one who got away. Now that I'm engaged, she seems to be the one that wants back in. A piece of me would love to have Summer back with me but I can't see myself without Alexis either.

Both are good women. Both really know me and love me anyway. Both are smart, fine and have a good sense of humor. Both women are the only two women whom I loved sleeping with above any other women in my life. I can see myself marrying and being happy with both of them. Now I'm stuck and don't know what to do.

I get out the shower, dry off and walk back into the room, where Alexis has passed out. I give myself a pat on the back for being able to put Alexis into a deep sleep so fast. I go to the dresser and pull out some boxers and a white under shirt. I pick up my pants from the side of the bed and pull out my cell phone and see that the light is blinking. I see that I have a text message from Summer.

It says: "I want you and you want me. Don't make the same mistake I made by walking away from us. We're meant to be. I love you, Honey."

I am not sure how to react or what to say. Summer has finally admitted she made a mistake in breaking up with me two years ago. Maybe she's finally come around and sees that she loves me as much

as I loved her. We were good
together when we were together.
And even as friends we were great. I
look over at Alexis who is letting out
some loud snores now and think
about where I see myself in the
future. Do I want kids with Alexis?
Can I grow old with Alexis? Will
Alexis be there with me through the
good and the bad? I don't know for
certain. What I do know is Summer
has already been there for me
through the good and the bad. She
helped me when I was struggling
through school, gave me advice on
love, and taught me how to make
love. Summer has always been
there and I can't imagine her not
being there. Even though we've
been apart for two years, she's
always been in my heart.

    I look back at the text message,
trying to figure out how to respond.
Do I tell her to get over me or do I
tell her to meet me in an hour? I
look back at Alexis who looks so
peaceful and beautiful. I don't want
to hurt her but I need to clear my
heart for either Alexis or Summer. I
go back to the text message and
type in a reply. "I want you. Let's
see if we're meant to be." I send the
text, then place my phone on the

charger that Alexis has put on the dresser for me.

I climb into bed and wrap my arms around Alexis and feel the heat from her body on mine. It feels good. She turns to the side so that her ass is into my stomach. I wrap my arm around to her breast and grab it. It's so soft and feels good in my hands. I hold Alexis tight as I drift off to sleep. I wonder if this is the last time I will hold Alexis. It's starting to seem that by the end of the weekend our engagement will be off and Summer will the one lying in bed next to me.

Chapter 16

Sean

I wake up to my cell phone ringing. I quickly hop out of bed to answer the phone hoping it's Summer calling. I grab the phone from the dresser, disappointed to see it's Eric. My first thought is to ignore the call and get back into bed but I change my mind.

"Hello."

"What up, family?" Eric says in an annoying happy tone.

I wanted to curse him out for waking me up early in the morning. I look at the clock on the nightstand next to the bed and see that it's eight 'o' clock. It's not too early, I guess but I was still tired. I look at Alexis who looks to still be asleep. She looks peaceful and beautiful. I've never seen a woman look more beautiful in the morning. It makes me want to get in the bed and get a second round in with her this morning. Thinking of that only makes me think of seeing Summer last night while we were having sex. The image of Summer made me get more aggressive and made the sex seem better.

"Sean, you there?" Eric asks.

"Yeah, I'm here, what's up?"

"Wanted to see if you wanted to grab breakfast with me this morning?"

"Just me and you?" I ask.

"Yeah. Wanted to talk to you about some stuff."

What is so important that he needs to talk to me about it this morning? It better not be any bull. I don't have time for any drama. Knowing Eric he probably wants to tell me about a new girl he met and how he thinks she may be better for him than Krystal. Eric always has some type of drama going on. That's one of the reasons he can't bring himself to marry Krystal. He always thinks there's something better out there for him.

"When you want to go?" I ask him.

"Man, I'll pick you up in ten minutes. I'm almost to your parents' place."

"Alright."

I hang up the phone and sit on the edge of the bed. Alexis sits up in the bed and stretches.

"Who was that?" She asks still yawning.

"Eric wants me to go to breakfast with him. Said he needed to talk to me about something." I tell her.

She gets out of the bed and walks to the bathroom and closes the door behind her. I go to the dresser and grab a pair of jeans and my blue button down shirt. I begin to put on my clothes when I hear the toilet flush and the water in the sink start to run. Alexis is brushing her teeth. Her morning ritual despite the fact we're not home.

I think about how well Alexis and I know each other. Our routines, our little quirks, our pet peeves and how we're able to deal with them. I love the fact that she is so routine because it keeps me in a routine and on a schedule. With Summer it was different every morning because every morning was spontaneous. Some mornings she may wake up and make breakfast and some mornings we'd be each other's breakfast. Alexis hasn't changed her routine once since we've been together.

As I finish getting dressed, Alexis walks out of the bathroom doing a yawn and stretch combo.

"How long do you think you'll be gone?" She asks.

I was expecting Alexis to ask if she could come. I was already trying to think of an excuse for her not to come, but I guess she already assumed she wasn't coming.

"I don't know, maybe an hour or two."

"Well, have fun with your friend. I'm going to go over the praise dance with your sister this morning."

"Okay" I say as I give her a kiss on the lips.

I walk to the bathroom to brush my teeth. Summer would have never let me kiss her first thing in the morning without brushing my teeth. She would tell me that my breath would get into her mouth and she didn't like the taste. Alexis doesn't seem to mind. After I brush my teeth and wash my face, I hear Eric's car pull in front of the house. Alexis is putting on a pair of jeans. I walk over to her and place my hand on her ass and kiss her neck. She turns to face me and kisses me on the lips.

"Have fun." She says as she kisses me again.

I leave out the private entrance of the transit apartment, close the door behind me and walk to Eric's Nissan Maxima. I get in the car and shake hands with Eric as he drives off.

"Sorry for the short notice, I just really needed to talk to you," he says as he turns down his music and makes a left on Linden St.

"What's up? It sounded hella important."

"Man, it's about Krystal."

"Don't tell me you cheated on her again.

Eric has cheated on Krystal a few times that I know of because I had to cover for him. I don't know why he did it, but he did and got away with it almost every time except once. A couple of years ago, after I moved to LA, Eric had no one to cover for him and he made the mistake of letting the girl spend the night at his house, knowing full well Krystal had a key. She caught him red handed. It took months for Krystal to forgive him.

"Man, I haven't cheated on Krystal since the last time she caught me at the house and pulled out that knife. I thought she was going to kill me or chop off my boys, which would have killed me anyway."

It's good Eric learned his lesson. Krystal may talk a bit too much but she is still a good woman and didn't deserve to be treated the way Eric treated her. So my next question would be if he hasn't cheated on her, what is the problem? I hope he's not thinking of breaking up with her.

We make it to the IHOP restaurant in Emeryville, which is just a few blocks from my parents' place. Eric finds a tight parking spot in the back of the building. We get out of the car and begin walking towards the restaurant. Eric locks the car with the push of a button. He then reaches into his black sports coat and pulls out a ring box and hands it to me.

I stop in my tracks as I look at the small black box in my hand. Eric stops and looks at me while adjusting his black slacks and straightening his yellow dress shirt. I can't even speak. A part of me wants to congratulate Eric on taking the next step. The other part of me wants to slap Eric and tell him that he could never turn in his player card.

"Is this what I think it is?" I ask already knowing the answer.

"Yeah, man, it is."

I shake my head as the two of us continue to walk into the IHOP. We are seated fast near a window towards the back of the restaurant. I finally open up the box and look at the ring. It's a nice size, at least two carats, but probably not totally flawless. I know if I couldn't afford totally flawless, Eric probably couldn't either. We make about the same amount per year.

"I bought it about three weeks ago; just been debating on giving it to Krystal," he tells me. He actually looks excited.

"Why you debating?" I ask him trying to get inside of his head.

If he bought this ring three weeks ago, he's obviously having second thoughts. I had the same feeling going through my head when I bought the ring for Alexis. I had the ring for only a few days, but if she hadn't found it, it may have been three weeks or more before I would have asked her to marry me.

"What if it's a mistake?" Eric says. His excitement is fading and the guy who is always joking is now serious.

The waitress comes and takes our order. I get the strawberry stuffed French Toast and Eric gets an order of pancakes. After the waitress takes our menus and walks away, I run down why Eric should ask Krystal to marry him. The first and obvious reason to me is she's pregnant. The second reason is they have been together for a long time. I explain to him that she has always had his back in everything and she is a ride-or-die type girl. She's faithful and above everything else, she loves him unconditionally.

"So you really think this is the right move?" Eric asks as our food arrives.

"Yeah, Eric. You need to wife this girl before somebody else comes along."

"Ain't no one else coming along. But I see what you saying."

We begin to eat and I ask Eric about Summer. He looks at me a little weird at first but then he understands where the conversation is going.

"You thinking about sleeping with Summer again, Sean?"

I look around to see if anyone heard him. No one seems to be paying any attention to our conversation so I nod.

"Summer is like a sister to me and I always liked you guys together, but man you're engaged now. Why would you mess it up?"

Eric makes a good point but he did also say he liked me and Summer together, which could be a sign that we are meant to be together.

"I don't think I can go and get married to Alexis if there is something still there for me and Summer."

"Sean, you know me. I'm always the one saying there is something better out there. So you do what you gotta do, Homie, and I have your back no matter what," Eric says as he finishes his meal.

As I get to the end of my French toast, I'm glad that at least Eric is on my side. He doesn't see anything wrong with me going after Summer as long as I'm happy. He's a true friend. I pull out my cell phone and text Summer: "Let's hook-up tonight". Less than a minute later I receive a reply from Summer: Let's. I don't really now what I'm doing, but I'm doing it.

Chapter 17

Alexis

I finish my morning quiet time with God and now I'm ready to start my day. My day always seems to go smoother when I pray and read the word. Today I got through chapters four and five of Ephesians. I paid special attention to chapter five where it talks about marriage and what the duties of a husband and wife are. A wife is to submit to her husband. To me this means being faithful and always having his back and always helping him reach his goals in life. It also talks about how a husband is supposed to love his wife like Christ loved the church and died for it. To me that means the husband should die to all other women and should be willing to do whatever he has to do to make his wife comfortable and happy. I hope and pray Sean is that man for me.

The smell of coffee and bacon reach my nose which lets me know breakfast is almost ready. Andrea came down a few minutes ago and told me Toni wanted me to join them for breakfast and I agreed. My mother always told me never to turn down a free meal. Toni and Andrea have made me feel so welcome. I have fallen in love with these two women and am excited they are going to be my family. I just hope Sean's father comes around too and soon.

I get a little nervous about going upstairs. What if Sean's father is there? What will I say to him or what will he say to me? I sit on the freshly made bed and think about what happened last night between Sean's father and me. He really offended me and the old me was ready to curse him out, but I knew I had to keep my cool. I definitely didn't want to start any drama in the house and that's exactly why I didn't say anything to Sean when he came home yesterday. It was tough, but I was able to convince Toni and Andrea not to say anything as well.

After the whole incident last night, I had a great conversation with Toni and Andrea. Toni kept apologizing on Ronald's behalf for his harsh words but I would rather hear the apology from him. There's no way a woman should have to apologize for her man's actions. He's grown and he should be man enough to admit when he's wrong. He need not only apologize to me, but also to his daughter whom he made cry. After Andrea had calmed down, Toni promised she would talk to Ronald about changing her major. Andrea felt a little relieved, but still didn't think anyone could persuade her father to change his mind because it was already set.

The conversation then turned to twenty questions about me and my life. They wanted to know everything about me, beyond the modeling and dancing, In an attempt to not over load them, I gave them the watered down version of my early life. I honestly felt if I told them too much they may think differently of me, or it may just bring the mood down too much. By the time Sean walked in the door last night, Toni and I had had a few wine coolers and were laughing along

with Andrea like we had known each
other for years.

After Sean finished his dinner
and went into the office to talk with
his father, Andrea asked about
Summer. She wanted to know if
Summer and I had crossed paths
yesterday. I told her we briefly saw
each other at Natalie's store.
Andrea spoke of her dislike for
Summer. She said Summer used
Sean, but for some reason Sean
didn't care or couldn't see it.
Andrea concluded with the fact she
was happy Sean found someone
who seems to really be in love with
her big brother. I assured her I am
crazy in love with Sean which made
Toni smile and begin to tear up.

My ringing cell phone breaks
my thoughts of last night. I get up
from my sitting position on the bed.
I grab the phone from the dresser
and answer Simone's call.

"Simone, you're up early."

"That's because I've been up all
night planning your wedding."

I laugh at my crazy cousin.
Simone isn't one to play around
when it comes to events. She has
actually been planning her own
wedding since she was twelve. Lord
only knows what she's got in store

for me. But she's moving a little too fast. It's barely been twenty-four hours since Sean and I got engaged.

"Cuz, we just got engaged less than two days ago. I haven't even set a wedding date yet."

"That's no problem. The wedding date is the third Saturday in June next year. It will be at our church and Pastor Tibbs will officiate. The color scheme will be purple and white and...."

I cut Simone off. "Hold on, Monie, don't I get a say in my own wedding? And what about Sean? He's not a fan of purple."

"All Sean has to do is stand at the alter and say 'I do'. As for you, all you have to do is find the right dress and I'll handle the rest."

"I appreciate the help, but lets discuss everything when I get home."

"You don't even want to know what kind of cake I picked out?" Simone asks, desperate to reveal her entire wedding plan.

"When I get home, Simone," I say with a little more sternness.

"Fine, I'll see you when you get back."

I end the call and place the phone in the back pocket of my tight jeans. I smile thinking about how good God is. I grew up with a sister who was so into herself that she never had time for me. If I tell her I'm getting married, she would make the whole thing about her. But Simone is looking out for me like a sister should. She knows purple is my favorite color and I've always dreamed of a wedding in a big church. Simone has been a blessing in my life.

I adjust my purple short sleeve top and walk up the stairs. I'm a little calmer and ready to handle what ever Sean's father has to say. I shouldn't be worried anyway; I just put on the whole armor of God. I'm ready for anything. The aroma of coffee and bacon gets even stronger on the second floor. Toni stands at the stove scrambling eggs, still in her robe and head wrap.

"Morning, Alexis. Breakfast is almost done."

I walk over to the coffee maker on the kitchen counter and grab one of the three cups in front of the freshly brewed coffee. I pour the coffee into the cup and add two teaspoons of sugar and powdered creamer, which is all set out.

"Is Mr. Winters joining us for breakfast?" I ask.

"No, he went down to the church to prep everything for tomorrow's anniversary."

I feel a bit relieved. I don't want to feel any tension at the breakfast table. I especially don't want any drama to mess up the nice spread Toni has prepared. She has bacon, toast, pancakes, fresh fruit and is just finishing up with the eggs.

Andrea comes out of her room in a chipper mood. She has changed from the pajamas she wore when I saw her a few minutes ago into a short yellow dress with black tights and a pair of black flats. She gives me a hug and her mother a kiss on the cheek. She then grabs a coffee cup and repeats everything I did except she uses three teaspoons of sugar.

Andrea and I sit at the table in front of plates full of food. Toni brings over the pan of eggs and divides them among the three plates on the table. She tosses the pan into the sink and pours cold water over it to cool it down. She then grabs her cup and pours coffee into it adding nothing. She sits at the table and smiles at the two women who are not her biological daughters. She tells me she feels a new responsibility with me after finding out my mother passed away. The same motherly responsibility she felt for Andrea after her mother died. I start to tear up. Toni doesn't say anymore about it. Instead we turn our focus to breakfast.

"Alexis, dear, can you bless the food."

I'm a little shocked at the request, but agree. We all bow our head as I thank God for bringing me into the Winters' family and for the love they have already shown. I bless the food and asked God to keep us all safe. The ladies say Amen and we dig in. As they eat, I look at Toni and Andrea, happy they accepted me into their family. Now I just want to stay in the family. I hope and pray Sean and I will make it through. I have a strange feeling Summer isn't going to make it easy. I know Summer wants Sean and that Sean still has feelings for Summer. I saw it when they looked at each other yesterday. I just hope Sean remembers he's engaged to me. Though when it comes to Summer, it may not matter.

Chapter 18

Summer

I lie in bed awake with a new attitude and a brand new mission. The text from Sean woke me up and it renewed my resolve to have him all to myself. I am going to prove to Sean I am the woman for him and I can be the perfect wife. I jump out of bed glad that I took two Excedrin's pills last night. The last thing I wanted to do was wake up with a hangover. I admit I went a little overboard with my drinking last night. Not my normal style, but I needed something to hide the pain of being alone.

I head to the bathroom and brush my teeth, wash my face and use the toilet before walking to my closet and picking out the perfect outfit to wear today. The weather report yesterday said it's supposed to be warm, so I pull out my blue jean skirt with a yellow short sleeve

V-neck top and my yellow and white heels. Sean is going to go crazy over this outfit. It shows off my smooth, thick legs, which lead up to my nice round ass. The shirt shows the right amount of cleavage to make any mans mouth water. The heels make my ass stand up and demand attention.

I get a little moist thinking about Sean putting his tongue on my nipples and then on my lips. I had one sex dream after another last night about Sean. He was either on top beating my walls into submission or I was riding him hard and fast. I must have climaxed at least three times. All I can think about now is making my dream a reality.

I take off my clothes and head back to the bathroom and turn on my shower. I want to make sure I am totally clean and fresh for my man. As I step into the shower, my mind goes back to my conversation with Natalie. I realize now that I made some huge mistakes with men in the past and the biggest one was hurting Sean.

I knew from a young age that I was a beautiful girl, the kind a lot of men liked. I was light skinned with

big juicy lips, big brown eyes, long
hair and a big booty. What can I
say; I get it from my mama. I saw
the way grown men looked at me
when I would walk down the street
and I have to admit I liked the
attention. When I got to high school
it seemed like all the boys wanted to
get with me so I had my pick of the
litter.

I liked athletes and Chris was
the best basketball player in the
district. I think I went after Chris
because unlike all the other guys in
school, Chris had all the girls after
him. It was more of a challenge to
make him mine. The only problem
was that he was never really all
mine. I caught him cheating several
times but I tried to ignore it. Prom
night was the last straw and I broke
it off with him. And Sean was there
to pick up the pieces. That is until I
started college and met Mark.

Like I said, I liked athletes and
Mark played football for Cal, drove a
Camero and had his own apartment.
The only thing Sean could offer me
was his old beat up car from high
school and his bedroom in his
parents' place. Sean had also
started to become more focused on
photography and less on me. To be

honest, I couldn't see Sean making any money in photography. He was good, but athletes, to me, were a sure thing. When I started seeing Mark I stopped sleeping with Sean. A few weeks later I heard he was dating a girl who modeled for him. I was slightly jealous but I couldn't be mad.

Mark proved to be too cocky and emotionally abusive. Nothing I did was ever right and he told me time and time again I was not that good in bed. This fool had the nerve to bring another girl to his apartment to show me how to give him head. That night I left him and went back to Sean.

At the time Sean was talking to a girl named Melanie. He told me it was nothing serious and broke it off with her to come back to my bed. After about three months I was at a party Eric was hosting and met Duncan, a third string player for the Raiders. He had money, muscles and looks. I couldn't help but fall in love. Again I told Sean we had to stop sleeping together. Sean was little annoyed with me but I knew he wouldn't stay mad for long. Especially if I could get him and Eric free tickets to the Raiders' games.

It was bittersweet with Duncan. He took me on trips, bought me jewelry, paid for my hair and nails to get done every other week and even bought me a Honda Accord. The problem was Duncan was abusive, physically. At first, it started with a pinch when I didn't come home at the appointed time. Then he started slapping me in the legs and on the arms, but never the face. He was extremely paranoid and constantly blamed me for cheating when I wasn't.

I tried to keep the abuse a secret, but Natalie saw a few bruises on my arm one day and called in the calvary. I tried hard to stop them, but Sean and Eric showed up to Duncan's house and promptly kicked his ass. I don't know what they said to him, but Duncan requested a trade and a few months later found himself in Atlanta. I found myself back in the protective arms of Sean who made me feel important again.

Life was good for about six months and Sean even confessed that he loved me. Even though Sean was good for me and my self-esteem, he was still broke and living with his parents.

As we approached the end of our fourth year in college, Sean and I didn't see each other much because of our schedules. When we did see each other we couldn't keep our hands off of one another. We were becoming booty calls. I didn't mind because it kept me from stressing out over my senior projects. It was hard to get together being that Sean was at Cal State East Bay in Hayward and I was across the bay in the dorms of the University of San Francisco.

During my last semester I got into a situation I shouldn't have. I took a class on human sexuality with the very fine, young professor Scott Hills. I made several office visits to professor Hills wanting help with assignments, but also wanting to be in his presence. One night while going over the study guide, professor Hills made his move and kissed me. I couldn't help but kiss him back. We made love in his office that night and every night thereafter for a week. We started meeting in hotels at his request. Our affair carried on for the rest of senior year and I had finally started to feel like I could love again. Then I found out professor Hills was married and had two kids.

When I confronted him about it he told me he was separated and planning on divorcing his wife and marrying me. I believed him when he said he was going to leave his wife but just wanted to make sure his young children were okay. I believed the lie until graduation and I got my bachelors degree in childhood development. At the graduation I saw the love between professor Hills and his wife, who was pregnant with their third child. Heart broken, I ended it with professor Hills and went back to my Sean. That was short lived because a few months later Sean moved to Los Angeles to be a professional photographer.

Then I was shocked. I had no idea that while Sean was driving around in that beat up car for the past eight years and living at home that he was saving a lot of money for his business venture. From doing part-time work in the mall and taking pictures for family and friends' special events, he had actually saved thousands of dollars. He was lightweight balling and I never knew. This revelation turned

me on and gave me motivation to
visit Sean once in a while.

Sean had been in LA for a year
before I met Nathan. Nathan
worked at a bank and coached little
league baseball on the weekends. I
had fallen hard for Nathan and was
ready to give my heart to him. I
wanted to give my heart to Sean but
he was hundreds of miles away. I
couldn't see doing the long distance
thing. It's one thing to visit every
few weeks and have a weekend sex-
a-thon, but it's another thing to be
monogamous with someone who
was not around. Nathan was tall,
dark and handsome and I really
wanted to see where things would
go. Before I went for it, I made one
more trip to LA to let Sean know I
met someone else.

A piece of me wanted to see if
Sean still loved me and that he may
want to make what he and I had
permanent. If Sean would have
asked me to stay with him, I would
have moved to LA and finished my
schooling there. I guess I was
looking for Sean to fight for me, but
he never did. Every time I told him I
met someone new he let me go
without a fight. I guess I just
figured he knew I'd always come

back to him. I was never able to go back to him after my last trip to LA.

When I got to LA that Friday night Sean was busy with work. He gave me the key to his place and told me to relax and make myself at home. So I did just that. I found some ground turkey in the freezer and some elbow macaroni in the cabinet. I did have to make a quick run to the store for some tomato sauce and seasonings. When I got back, I made a casserole, green beans, dinner rolls and a salad.

When Sean got home he enjoyed the meal I prepared and he enjoyed me for dessert. As I lay on my back with him deep sea diving, I realized how happy I was. I made dinner for Sean and was now being pleasured by the only man who truly knew my body inside and out.

He ate me and I returned the favor. He always loved my oral pleasure. We went at it like two wild animals. There seemed to be extra passion between us. He pounded my walls into submission. I rode him until he couldn't hold on anymore and we climaxed together. Sean brought me to climax several times that night. He pleased me in every possible way. Our lovemaking was always perfect. I never had a complaint when it came to Sean Winters. He was blessed with looks, pipe and now money. I wanted to make him mine but I always questioned if he would fight for me.

The next morning, after we had slept in each other's arms, I got up and made breakfast. While Sean ate his French toast, eggs and sausage, I informed him of Nathan. I told him about how Nathan was a good guy and treated me nice. I don't know what it was but I really wanted to make Sean jealous. I wanted him to propose to me and tell me that he doesn't want me to be with anyone but him. He told me he loved me. I wanted him to prove it, but he did the opposite.

"So you just came here to put it on me and then go back to this new guy?" Sean asked in between bites.

"What, are you jealous? You want me to stay with you?" I asked while taking a sip of coffee.

"You do what you want to do, Summer. You always have," Sean said as he got up from the table and put his empty plate in the sink.

A little hurt and offended by Sean's comment, I chose not to say anything.

Sean walked over and kissed me on the forehead. "I've got to get to work. If you're leaving, leave the key under the mat. Otherwise I'll see you later."

And with that Sean grabbed his camera bag and left without saying goodbye. At the time, I thought Sean's behavior was uncalled for. I did give him the opportunity to ask me to stay and he didn't. I was a little more than pissed that he didn't even seem to care. So I got up, washed the dishes, packed my bags and left his key under the mat and traveled back to Oakland to be with Nathan.

I actually thought if Sean wasn't the one for me then maybe Nathan was. But after only six months the relationship with Nathan fizzled because of our schedules. With him working everyday and coaching on the weekends and me in medical school and getting ready to apply for internships the next year, we never had time for each other. It was a mutual decision and neither one of us were mad. I was a little sad because Nathan was a good man. He just wasn't the one for me.

After the break-up with Nathan, I focused solely on medical school and getting an internship with Kaiser Permanente in San Francisco. During a short break in classes, I realized it had almost been a year since I had talked to Sean. He hadn't called me and I was too busy to call him. I heard updates from Eric and Natalie and knew he started dating a model but didn't know how serious it was. I got my internship with Kaiser and was doing great in school, but I hadn't had sex in close to six months after breaking up with Nathan. I decided that since I had a few days to relax I would go down to LA and get my freak on with Sean and then come back and get back to business.

When I called Sean to let him know I was coming down, he told me he was dating Alexis. That didn't bother me. I still wanted Sean to be inside of me. I told him that Alexis would never know and it would be just like old times. But Sean told me the heartbreaking news that Alexis now had a key to his place and that they were practically living together. I didn't realize he and Alexis were so serious. And in my heart I just knew Sean would come back to me so I told him to call me when the relationship with Alexis had run its course. Obviously it never did and he never called.

With a little hurt from the rejection from Sean, I quickly got into a casual relationship with Jackson, a sports agent out of San Francisco. He and I met while shopping at Stonestown mall. We both had hectic schedules. Jackson traveled a lot and I was just about to enter my residency at Kaiser. But somehow we made it work for over a year. Jackson even proposed, but then the secret phone calls started and Jackson made the mistake of not cleaning his condo very well. I started finding jewelry that wasn't mine. I even found a pair of boy shorts; I wear hip huggers and thongs. Jackson finally came clean about his multiple affairs and promised after we got married it would all stop. I had played the fool before with professor Hills and I was not going to do it twice. I broke it off with Jackson and have been single for the past few months.

My daydream of boyfriends past ends and I am now dressed and ready for the day. I finish applying my make-up and wonder if Natalie is right. Maybe I just want to be with Sean because it has been a few months since I got some. No. I want to be with Sean because out of all the guys I have ever dated, he is the only one to make me feel safe, protected and truly loved. I have been hurt too many times and I'm ready to have a man I know won't hurt me. Sean has always been my man and now I need to make him see that before he makes a huge mistake and marries the wrong woman.

I have no problem with Alexis as a person, but there is no way Alexis can love Sean the way that I can. There's no way Alexis can sex Sean the way I can either. I know him because I trained him. We experimented together. I was his first and I'm damn sure going to be his last.

"It's time to take back what's mine." I say to my reflection in the mirror.

Looking at myself in the mirror and thinking about Sean putting a pounding on my kitty has got me anxious. Tonight is too long to wait. I want Sean now. I walk out the bedroom and grab my cell phone from the charger in the dining room and dial in Sean's number. I already have a plan set. By this time tomorrow Alexis will be heading back to LA with tears in her eyes and Sean will be in my arms forever. The image of Sean in my bed makes me smile. Finally Sean answers the phone on the fourth ring.

"Hey, Honey, it's me. I need to see you right now. Come to my place."

Chapter 19

Sean

I hang up the phone with Summer. She sounds like she really wants to see me. But I'm not in my car, I'm still with Eric.

"What was that about, Family?" Eric asks.

"It's Summer. She said she needs to see me right away."

Eric shakes his head as he turns onto San Pablo. "What you want to do?"

I'm not sure. Eric was still nervous about asking Krystal to marry him so he wanted to kill some time by going to Best Buy and possibly getting some new electronics. Then he wanted to hit up Office Max and get some supplies for his office. "I'm kicking it with you man. I'm trying to get you ready for your big proposal tonight."

"Man I can handle it. I'll drop you over at Summer's real quick, do what I have to do and come back in an hour to get you."

I look at Eric for a second considering his offer. "You're an enabler, Bruh."

Eric nods and smiles. "Yes I am."

"Alright, let's swing by Summer's, but you stay in the car and wait for me."

"There you go, acting like the Sean I always wanted you to be. Go get you a little quickie and be back to your woman before she misses you."

I just shake my head and think about all the side women Eric had back in the day. He'd always have one main girl but at least three other women he could call to get a fix when his main wasn't acting right. The boy was a down right playa and I wouldn't be surprised if he still had a woman or two on the side now. It was always hard for me to juggle more than one woman at a time. Every time I tried I ended up getting caught after a few weeks. But Eric was slick. He never got caught, that is, until he met Krystal. Maybe that's why he's ready to marry her. Krystal is the only woman Eric couldn't fool or get to believe his lies. She sees right through him.

As Eric drives down 45th past Telegraph towards Broadway, I think about what I'm doing. I can't shake the feeling that this is a bad decision on my part. If Alexis knew what I was doing she would be pissed. But she is the one who told me to confront my feelings for Summer. How else am I suppose to know how I really feel about Summer unless I talk with her, kiss her, sleep with her? I need to know if the fire is still burning between us. I need to know if Summer is truly the one for me.

As Eric parks in front of Summer's condo, my nerves start to get to me. I have a feeling that when I go up to Summer's place I'm not going to be able to help myself. We came close to kissing last night and I don't know if a phone call can stop me if our lips come that close again. I look to Eric who is all smiles, because he knows what's on my mind. He's thinking, "go up there and get you some then come back down and give me all the details."

"Go on, Sean. What you waiting on? You already got the invitation."

I look at Eric and nod my head. I get out of his car and head for Summer's condo. Walking to the front door, I imagine Summer opening the door wearing nothing but high heels, black or red, doesn't matter. She'd done that a few times when I would come over to her apartment while we were in school. She would tell me she needed help with something to get me over to her place and when I'd ring the bell she would open the door butt naked except for a pair of black heels. One time we forgot to close the door and a neighbor saw the whole thing. It was little embarrassing, but the female neighbor did clap for us when we were through. And when I left she made sure to slip me her number, which I never used. Well, I did once after Summer moved out. But nothing happened, she'd gotten engaged.

I ring the doorbell and a few seconds later Summer opens the door. She is wearing a skirt with a yellow top that shows off her cleavage. She also has on some intoxicating perfume that makes me rise a bit. She looks me up and down stopping for a longer look at my bulge. She bites her bottom lip and stares at what she wants. She breaks her stare then steps away from the doorway to let me in and closes the door behind me.

I look at her and lick my lips. This woman drives me crazy. No matter how hard I try to deny it, all I want to do is be inside of her. I feel myself rising so I try to change my thinking, but it's too late. She sees and likes what she sees.

"Don't get all excited, Honey, I just said I need to talk to you." Summer walks past me to her love seat and sits.

I stand trying to will myself to go down. After a few seconds of thinking about business I feel myself shrinking back. Summer motions for me to sit next to her.

"You know what almost happened last night when we sat next to each other?"

"Yeah, you left." She pats the love seat again.

I walk to the love seat and sit. Her perfume turns me on again. I look at this sexy woman sitting next to me as she smiles. She knows she finally has me and this time I won't leave. I am totally at her mercy and I don't mind. I want to kiss her lips, then her neck, then her tits, then her naval, then her lips. I want to taste every part of her. I want to make her scream my name as I go deeper and deeper inside her walls. And I know she wants it too.

"You left in such a hurry last night, we didn't get a chance to really talk." She begins.

"Wasn't sure if we were making a mistake last night." I tell her.

I wasn't sure. I mean every part of me wants to sex Summer down but is that the only thing between us now, a physical attraction? It's been two years since we've been together. Is that too much time? I've always loved Summer, from the moment she moved across the street from me. Summer was there for me when I found out about The Good Reverend Winters' affair. She calmed me down when all I wanted was to destroy something, hit something, curse out my father.

Summer would help me when I was struggling to pass classes in high school and college. She would always help me study even though she had a crazy class schedule herself. Most of all, Summer never ceased to surprise me in the bedroom. She'd pull out some new trick that would drive me crazy. Yes, sex with Summer was always awesome.

But now I'm thinking, what else besides the great sex was the attraction to Summer? Besides the fact that she is beautiful, what else did she really have to offer? The more I think about the good times we had, the more I think about the bad times. Summer actually hurt me every time she broke it off with me to be with someone else. I tried not to be insecure but I always felt like I wasn't good enough for her. I was just something to do until someone she really liked came along.

Trying to hide my hurt, I would just start dating girls I really didn't care about. I'd sleep with them but had no emotional connection to them. They were just something to do until Summer came back around. And as soon as Summer did come back to my bed, those other girls were gone, distant memories. It's sad when I think about it, but I don't remember some of their names because when Summer was with me, no one else mattered. But now someone else does matter. Alexis, my fiancée.

Summer puts her hand on my leg. "You wanted to know if I really loved you or if being with me would be like all the other times?"

Trying to keep myself from rising again, I simply nod trying to think of other things.

She continues. "I realize that it seemed that I was using you, but I wasn't. Or at least I wasn't trying to. I was young and dumb and wanted to explore. I needed more experiences. I didn't want to be settled at seventeen years old."

Summer goes on to explain that she knew I would always be around because I was a good and loyal man. She says she needed to date the other men in order to know for sure she had the right man in me. She goes on to tell me that she wished I fought harder for her and not let her go. A tear falls from her eye as she tells me that she is sorry for hurting me each time she broke it off with me for another man.

"I can't see being with any other man now, Sean. I love you and I'm sorry I didn't see it before." Tears fill her eyes. "I would die if you weren't in my life anymore. It's been killing me the past two years not being with you."

I wipe the tears from her eyes as I try to hold back my own. I have never heard Summer talk this passionately about anything other than becoming a pediatrician. I was not prepared for her to cry and to say that she can't live without me. Could it be true? The woman I have been after for half my life finally wants me and only me. I kiss her forehead then her cheek.

I whisper in her ear, "I've always loved you, Summer."

She turns her head and looks me directly in the eyes. "Then prove it and make love to me."

She kisses me. Her soft lips suck on mine. I kiss her back, passionately. She glides her soft tongue into my mouth and my tongue dances with hers in perfect harmony. She climbs on top of me and straddles my lap. I put my hands on her nice, round ass as she grinds against my manhood. I squeeze on her cheeks as our kissing becomes more aggressive and our breaths more labored.

Summer puts my head on her breasts and I inhale her perfume, which she sprayed right in the middle. "Yes, Sean. Do it, Honey."

As I kiss her neck, my mind wanders to the Good Reverend Winters and his affair years ago. I think about how much it hurt my mother and how I never wanted to hurt a woman I loved like that. Then I think about Alexis and how much I do love her. If she knew what I was doing right now, it would break her heart. But I'm fighting a losing battle because the wrong head wants to do the thinking right now.

Summer jumps off of my lap and drops to her knees. She begins to pull at my belt. She unbuckles it and then unbuttons my pants. I'm hard and ready for whatever she wants to do right now, but I can't get Alexis out of my head. It's almost like she's haunting me right now. Summer grabs my manhood in her hand. She smiles as she begins to pull it through my boxers and out into the world.

I stop her. I grab her hand and pull it off of me. She looks confused and stands.

"What's wrong, Honey? You love when I give you a blow-your-mind blow job."

I stand and zip up my pants
and buckle my belt. "I can't do it.
Not right now at least."

"Are you still thinking about
Alexis?" She asks standing herself.

"She is my fiancée."

Summer gets annoyed. "I just
poured my heart out to you and
professed my eternal love to you and
you still want to go back to her?"

"Look, Summer, if the two of us
are going to be together then I have
to let Alexis know. It's only fair.
And if we're going to be together,
you need to think about what you
want to do. Are you going to move
to LA with me or what?"

"Why think about that now?
I'm horny as hell and all I want is
that big stick inside of me. We can
make all the plans and break all the
hearts after a round or two or
three."

Summer's last statement
makes me think that maybe she is
just lonely and in need of sex.
Perhaps she doesn't love me as
much as she says or thinks she
does. If she really wanted to be with
me, she would have thought about
everything and not just getting me
in bed She needs to do a little more

thinking and we should talk a little more before we sleep together.

"I'm sorry, Summer, but if I'm going to break Alexis' heart, I need a reason other than you wanting to have sex."

Summer slaps me in the chest. "I just told you I love you! What else do you need?"

"We've said I love you to each other a ton of times and you still dated other men."

"Sean, you've dated other women. What's the difference?"

I gently put my hands on her shoulders. "The difference is that I never broke up with you to date those other women. I only dated them after you broke it off with me."

"And I apologized," she says with tears coming down her cheek.

I wipe the tears away. "I know. But you've burned me too many times."

Summer pushes my hands away, shakes her head and bites her lip. "The past is the past. I'm trying to start over with a future for me and you."

I know the past is the past, but the past keeps coming to my present thoughts like a still photograph. They say a picture is worth a

thousand words but memories are
worth millions more. I can't shake
the memories of Summer coming to
me and coming with me, then telling
me that she met someone new and
couldn't sleep with me anymore.

After the last time she came to
my condo, made me dinner, then
sexed me like never before, I
thought that she was finally ready to
commit to me. I was finally ready to
commit. My career was taking off.
I had my own home and was getting
ready to buy a new car. The only
thing I needed was a good woman by
my side and I hoped it was Summer.

Summer waited until the next
morning over breakfast to tell me
she met someone new. I was so
pissed. I wanted to curse her ass
out or strangle her for leading me to
believe she was mine for good. But I
just left. A piece of me hoped she
would be in my condo when I
returned home that night, but I
wasn't surprised when I found she
was gone. That night I did a lot of
thinking and decided I was not
going to let Summer continue to
come in and out of my life anymore.
I prayed that God would send me a
good woman who would not leave

me like Hosea's wife did him in the Bible.

A few weeks later I met Alexis and have been happy ever since. But now I'm allowing Summer back into my heart and I can't stop it. I have so much love for her that I'm willing to let her hurt me. Not this time. I can't let her continue to use me for good sex then leave without giving it a second thought when the next rich man comes along.

Summer breaks my train of thought. "What's is going to be, Sean Winters? A future with your first and true love or a future with the video vixen?"

"Let me talk to Alexis tonight and then I can tell you where I'm at."

"So you're going to leave me here horny again?" Summer says with her hands on her hips.

The head on my shoulders says yes but the head between my legs says no I'll give it to you right now on your love seat. I lick my lips and she smiles, knowing what I'm thinking. She is so damn sexy, but it's like she's the forbidden fruit and I can't help but have a bite. I look her up and down. She walks to me and puts her hands around my waist. She then takes one hand and puts it on my manhood.

"He wants me, Sean. Don't deny him. I know he's missed me."

I become weak as she squeezes me and awakens me. "Hold on till tonight. Everything should be settled," I tell her.

Summer pouts and gives me puppy dog eyes. She then nods and kneels down and kisses me though my jeans. "I'll see you later tonight." She stands up straight and kisses me soft on my lips, invading my mouth with her tongue. "I'll see you both tonight."

I walk to the door trying to fight the urge to rip off Summer's clothes and beat her walls up with straight jabs. As I get to the door I turn to Summer. She smiles then lifts her shirt and bra up and flashes me. Her firm tits stand at attention. Her brown nipples look at me and almost put me in a trance. I open the door and make a quick exit.

Trying to shake the thoughts running through my head, wrap my head around the fact that for the second straight time I've walked away from free sex. This time Summer was about to blow my mind but I stopped her. Even though

281

Alexis didn't call this time, it was like she was talking to me. I just kept thinking about her and how the men she's been with have done her wrong and I don't want to be like every other guy. In the same instance, Summer has had some of the same luck with men and I have always been her safe haven. I don't want to hurt her either.

The problem is that no matter what, before this weekend is over, one of them is going to be hurt and I'm going to be the cause. Summer has always been the one I wanted from day one and I think she's finally ready to commit to me. Alexis is the woman who came into my life and made things make sense. She made me see that I don't have to live in fear of her leaving me for another man. She loves me.

I'm so deep in thought that I didn't realize that I walked past the guest parking area. I notice that Eric's car isn't there. This bastard left! I pull out my cell phone and see that I have a text message. It's from Eric saying that he went to Best Buy and Office Max and would be back in about an hour and for me to have fun.

"Damn, now how am I going to get to my parents' house?" It's a pretty long walk even though it's about five minutes in a car. I should call Eric and have him come back and get me but that may take a while.

Suddenly a car pulls up on the side of me. "You need a ride?" Summer asks.

"Yeah, it seems like my ride left me."

'You know Eric. He's not one for waiting."

I open the passenger door and get into Summer's BMW. She smiles at me and drives off. I'm glad I have ride now and don't have to walk, but something doesn't feel right. It doesn't seem like a good idea to pull up in front of my parents' house in Summer's car.

Chapter 20

Alexis

After breakfast and a long talk with Toni and Andrea, I helped clean the kitchen then agreed to help Andrea wash her car. I feel at peace standing in the driveway on this warm summer day I feel at peace. I know I still need to find a way to be accepted by Sean's dad, but I believe it will happen in time. It had only been a day and Toni and Andrea made me feel like family. That's something I haven't had in a long time.

"All done." Andrea says as she finishes drying the front window of her little Honda Civic.

"Looks good," I say, as we both admire the pretty red vehicle.

"So, do you have an idea of how you want the wedding day to be?" Andrea asks as she pours the bucket of soapy water out into the street.

"I just want something simple. I don't have a lot of family. I know my big sister will come and I have a few relatives in LA." I tell her as I take the two dry towels and hang them on the railing of the stairs leading to the house.

Andrea sets the bucket next to the stairs and wipes her hands on her pants. "I want a big wedding."

"You have some prospects?" I was curious. I have not heard Andrea talk about boys at all since we've been in town.

Andrea shakes her head. "I've been single for a while. I broke up with my last boyfriend about six months ago. He was trying to be too aggressive about having sex."

I look at Andrea in shock. "Are you still a virgin?"

Andrea puts her finger to her lips to quiet me. "Don't say it so loud. The last thing I need is for Mom to hear and start asking a bunch of questions. Then my dad will start giving me the birds and bees talk. Although his was called boys, girls and God."

I laugh. Still a little shocked. I didn't know anybody that stayed celibate through high school. I am sure Andrea will have an experience or ten in college. All I heard about college was it was an all day sexcapade. I can't stop staring at Andrea. I'm trying to figure out how she was able to withstand all the advances she surely gets. She's a pretty girl and she's smart. I am certain boys are after her all the time.

"Don't look at me like I'm an endangered species," Andrea says noticing my stare.

"I'm just surprised."

"Don't be. My body, my decision. My dad always said if a man isn't willing to wait for it, he doesn't deserve to have it."

I nod in agreement. I think about Sean and me and how he patiently waited for me and how it had been the best decision either one of us could make. The wait made everything so much more special. Waiting actually allowed us to learn each other and fall in love with each other and not in lust with each other. I was totally in love with Sean before we became intimate with each other.

My sweet memories are broken by the sound of R&B music coming down the street. A silver BMW pulls in front of the house and Sean is in the passenger seat. To my surprise, Summer is in the driver's seat. Now my mind begins to race because Sean left with Eric this morning. I saw him get into Eric's car, so how in the hell did he end up in Summer's?

I look at Andrea to see if she sees the same thing I see. Andrea has her mouth wide open and her eyes bugged out. I look back to the car just in time to see Summer give Sean a kiss on the cheek. Sean tries to avoid it but it's too late. Sean quickly gets out of the car and walks towards the driveway.

Summer rolls down the window and says, "Bye, Honey." She then gives me a wink and a devilish grin and pulls into her parents' driveway across the street. She gets out of the car and goes into the house using her own key.

Sean walks to me. "Hey, Lexis."

Sean leans in for a kiss, but I move away from him, trying my best not to yell and slap the taste out of his mouth. I feel my anger boiling and am ready to say the first four-letter word that comes to mind. How dare Sean show up to the house in Summer's car, especially when he was suppose to be having breakfast with Eric? He's got a lot of explaining to do and he better do it quickly before I find something to hit him with!

"You're an idiot." Andrea says.

Sean tries to play it off. "What?"

"If you don't know what, big brother, then you need to put yourself in Alexis' shoes. See how you would react if she showed up at your house in the car of an ex who kisses her and calls her honey."

"Quit trippin', Summer's a friend."

"Like I said, you're an idiot." Andrea grabs her keys off of the stairs, hops in her Honda, starts it up and drives off before Sean can say anything else.

Sean looks at me and I know he can sense I'm pissed. I am trying to tell myself I didn't see what I so obviously saw. But I can't erase the wink and the smile. It's the same wink and smile Summer gave me yesterday at Natalie's store. I have been wondering who the wink was for at the store, but now I know it was directed at me. Game recognizes game. Summer was working on a plan to get Sean, and from the looks of it, she might have succeeded. Sean's clothes look a little ruffled. There is a dark spot on his blue shirt, which could be make-up, and he smells like perfume that I don't wear. Obviously they were close, and recently. I fight the urge to pull down Sean's pants and do a sniff test.

"Lexis, nothing happened, okay." Sean tries to break the icy cold silence.

I stay and speak in a calm tone. "I thought you went to breakfast with Eric."

"I did."

Trying to keep from yelling and making a scene that would bring Sean's mom out and possibly some neighbors, I choose my words wisely. "Then tell me, fiancée, how is it that you were just dropped off by your ex-girlfriend?"

I can see Sean's mind racing trying to figure out the perfect lie to tell me. I don't understand why men try to lie knowing the truth will eventually come out. There is nothing that is done in the dark that doesn't come to the light. I've kept my calm demeanor for the past few minutes, but if Sean lays to me, I will definitely let him have it. There is nothing I dislike more in this world than a liar. If I can just meet one man that doesn't lie, then maybe I'll find the perfect man.

"You going to answer me or do you not have your lie straight yet?" I ask in a calm yet stern tone, after he doesn't respond to my inquiry.

Sean breaks down and tells me the whole story of how he went and saw Summer last night and they started to talk but ended up arguing. Then he tells me about how after breakfast Summer called him and asked him to come over so they could talk again. He told me Eric was supposed to wait and the conversation would be short. He explains they came close to having sex, but he stopped and left. Eric was gone when he came out and while he was walking away from the condo, Summer offered him a ride and he accepted it.

I listened, not saying a word, with my anger building and building. Sean cheated on me. He didn't have sex with Summer, but wanted to in his heart and that's just as bad. A piece of me can't blame him because I'm at fault too. I told Sean to confront his feelings with Summer. I pushed my man into the arms of another woman.

I'm not sure what to think or feel right now. I'm angry with Sean for kissing another woman. I'm also mad at myself for telling him to go to Summer. Why couldn't I just be satisfied with the fact Sean put the ring on my finger? I just can't see marrying him if his heart is somewhere else.

"Baby, say something." Sean says trying to get a reaction out of me.

"You were going to sleep with her?"

Sean nods. "I was, but I thought about hurting you and couldn't do it."

"Should have thought about me before you made the decision to go to her house last night. If at the first argument you're going to run to your ex, then what's the point of marrying me?"

Sean puts his hands around my waist. "Because I love you and want to be with you. I made a mistake, but I'm admitting it and trying to move on."

I move Sean's hands away and just stare at him. My eyes begin to fill with tears but I won't let them fall. I've done enough crying over men in my life and I'm not doing it anymore. I think about how good of a man Sean has been to me, faithful all the way, until today. Now I'm seeing him like all the other men in my past. They all cheat. Sean had just not had the right person to cheat with until now.

"Is she out of your system?"

Sean nods. "I think so."

I roll my eyes. "Not good enough." I take my ring off and hold it out for Sean. "You can give it back if and when you're sure."

Sean shakes his head. "You're not leaving me that easy. I waited a long time for you, you're mine." He says sternly. He kisses me on the forehead and lightens his tone. "We'll get through this."

Sean hugs me and I hug him back. I look over Sean's shoulder at the house across the street and see Summer standing in the front window smiling. Summer takes her thumb and wipes the corners of her mouth, then winks at me. She then closes the blinds of the front window. I feel like running across the street, breaking down the door and throwing that tramp through the window. Sean breaks the hug and takes the ring from my hand and places it back on my finger. I start to pull away but decide against it. I love Sean and I still want to marry him, but I'm afraid I'm setting myself up for heartbreak.

"This is yours for forever." Sean kisses me gently. "Lets go inside."

I melt at his voice and obey his request. We walk into the apartment under the main house. Sean closes the door and leads me to the bed. He kisses me again and picks me up in his arms. I don't fight it even though I want to. Sean places me gently on the bed. He unbuttons my pants and pulls them down. Next he pulls down my boy shorts. He then proceeded to please me.

He kisses my lips then allows his tongue to find my pearl. He lightly caresses it causing me to begin the forgiving process. As Sean kisses, licks and sucks, I begin to feel more like Sean is telling the truth and that he really wants me and not Summer. I give in and allow Sean to bring me to climax. The anger and tension has been replaced by pure ecstasy.

Sean rises and wipes his chin, which is dripping with juices. He lays down on the bed next to me and holds me in his arms. I turn towards him and place my head on his rock hard chest and listen to his heartbeat, which always clams me down. Sean takes his hand and rubs my back, comforting and relaxing me. Hanging on to my anger would be pointless right now. At this moment I am the one lying next to Sean in nothing but a T-shirt and socks.

"I love you." I finally break our silence.

"I love you too," Sean responds and kisses my forehead.

Trying to get my mind off of the incident that just happened with Summer, I talk about something totally different. Trying to figure out what else to talk about is killing me because all I can think about is Sean kissing Summer and nearly sleeping with her. I take comfort in the fact he stopped and tried to leave. But, I can't shake the fact he put himself in that situation in the first place. He should have never let it get that far. Feeling my anger resurfacing, I decide to make light of my run in with Sean's dad.

"Your dad is quite a character."

"Oh, yeah, he says something last night?" Sean asks.

I tell Sean the whole story, starting from Andrea wanting to go to dance school and move to LA. I tell him about Andrea being scared of her dad and how I had to go with Andrea to talk to him about her dream. I try hard to turn it into a funny story by telling Sean how his dad got so angry and that he forbade Andrea to become a woman who sales sex like her.

"Wait a minute." Sean sits up in anger while I try to laugh it off. "Are you saying my dad called you a ho?"

Feeling I made a mistake telling Sean the story, I sit up and place a hand on his chest to calm him down. The fire in Sean's eyes right now makes me think I may have to return the favor he just gave me to keep him calm. "No, he just doesn't understand what I do."

"So he feels he can just dictate what Andrea can do with her life and disrespect you without anybody saying anything?"

I can see it 's going to take more than my touch or a BJ to calm my man down. "No, your mother gave him a tongue lashing last night."

Sean stands. "He's at the church, right?"

I stand still half naked and dripping a bit. "I think so, but I told you there's nothing left to say to him. I'm over it."

Sean heads for the door. "Oh, I'm not going to go talk to him, I'm going to do what I should have done years ago. I'm going to kick his ass."

Sean has an anger in his eyes that I've never seen before. It was the kind of rage I saw in my ex drug dealer boyfriend the day I saw him beat someone nearly to death for grabbing my ass in a club. It's the kind of rage you get when you want to kill someone.

I wanted to calm him down. Here I am standing in front of him with easy access to my paradise and all he has to do is fall in. I want him to, but his anger is too far gone. Nothing is going to calm him. It's not the comment that made him so angry, but the comment was the last straw. Sean didn't say another word. He just walked out of the small apartment and headed down the street to his father's church. All I can do is watch. I can't run after him because I don't have on any

pants. I say a quick prayer and
start getting dressed.

Chapter 21

Sean

The heat of the afternoon and the walk down to the church made me even angrier. I can't believe The Good Reverend Winters thinks he can just say whatever he wants without any consequences. He's always so quick to judge people before he knows them and his assumptions about them are usually wrong. But now he's gone too far because he's judging the woman I plan to marry. He has no right to tell her that her job is to sell sex. Her pictures are always tasteful. Her video dancing is art and choreographed most times by her.

Just when I thought things might get better between us, he goes and pulls something like this. He talked to me last night and never once mentioned his words with Alexis. He got me to forgive him when he disrespected my woman an hour or so before. I almost cried with him last night, letting all my anger and disappointment dissipate after such a long time. Now he's going to feel my wrath. I'm going to kick his ass in his own damn church.

I walk up to the big, green church doors and walk in. The place looks totally different from the last time I visited about five years ago. There are holes in the walls and ceiling. The paint is faded and peeling. The red carpet is all torn up and has stains all over. My anger turns to sympathy as I walk throughout the medium sized church.

I walk to the kitchen and see the same old appliances and dishes I remember from my childhood. Nothing has been updated. Not the refrigerator, stove, nor the counter tops, everything is the same. There are ants crawling all over the place. It looks sad and definitely not a place where I would ever want to eat.

I walk to the bathroom that appears to have leaks at the sinks. The toilets look as if they haven't been cleaned in weeks. I turn the hot water knob on the sink but it doesn't turn on. The cold water does, however, come on with weak pressure. A cheap bar of hand soap sits on the sink with hair and dirt mixed in it. The smell of dried piss and sweat invades my nostrils as I look into the two bathroom stalls.

I walk of the bathroom into the lobby. I go through the double doors that lead into the sanctuary. The doors are uneven and don't close all the way. The carpet looks the same as in the lobby. The dark brown pews look old and chipped. Some of the pew benches are broken. The sanctuary could actually hold about four to five hundred. I walk to the pulpit where an old podium with an attached microphone sits. Behind the podium sit three chairs. Two small chairs and one large chair in the middle. Behind the chairs on a raised stage sits five rows of pews for the choir.

This is definitely not the picture of perfection I expected to see when I walked into the church today. I remember as a kid it being vibrant and full of life. The paint always looked good. The carpet never had a stain. How could The Good

Reverend Winters let this happen to the church? It looks like some type of abandoned building with working lights. It doesn't make sense. One thing my father was when I was a kid, was anal about was how his church looked on the inside and out. I was too mad to notice the outside, but the inside slapped me in the face.

This is not the perfect image of God's house. It has been five years since I've stepped foot in a church. Alexis goes every Sunday she's in town, faithfully. Just knowing that the man who was supposed to be our example could sin made me think that every Preacher was a hypocrite. My father turned me against preachers and so called leaders of the church, but not against God.

It seems like every few weeks I hear about another scandal in the church. Preachers are always getting in trouble for sleeping with members, or stealing money, or using drugs. I've even heard churchgoers say some preachers just teach the word wrong and are only in the pulpit for show. And if my father, who was my hero, could fail to do right, how can I expect any other so called men of God to do right?

My thing is that I will keep my relationship with God between the two of us and stay away from the church. I feel its helped me because things have been going great in my life. I have everything I can possibly want right now. But if I have gained everything and my father has lost everything, I've gained nothing. Despite my anger for what he did to my mother, my father was always a good provider. He took care of me. He paid my bills when I didn't have money. He paid for school the whole way so I didn't have to use financial aid. He even put a little money towards getting my studio started. I raised about twenty thousand from working part-time and doing pictures for people on the side while I was in school. It was my father, however, who co-signed the loan that helped me get all equipment and start up cash I needed to run the studio. Looking at the church, I feel it's my turn to take care of my old man and his dream, because it looks as if it has all fallen apart. I walk to the back of the church towards the stairs that lead to the administration offices. Three small offices sit on the second floor. One being the finance office, which my mother runs. The second being the assistant minister's office, though I don't think my father has an assistant minister at the moment. The third office is, of course, The Good Reverend Winters' office. There is also a small conference room set up for meetings and small Bible study classes.

As I walk up the stairs, I hear my father's voice, but can't make out who he's talking to. As I get closer to his office, I realize he's not just talking, he's praying. His voice sounds shaky and almost as if he's praying and crying at the same time. I don't want to be rude and eavesdrop on his conversation with God, but I can't help but hear what he has to say. I walk slowly and quietly towards his office door and see him sitting at his desk, his chair turned to face the wall.

"Father, I thank you for all that you've done. I thank you for bringing my son this weekend. I hope that we can begin to rebuild our relationship. I pray that Alexis is the woman you have selected for

him and that she would be a good
wife and friend for him. And then,
Father, I ask that you allow this
anniversary set for tomorrow to go
off without a hitch. I know that
things haven't looked so good for the
last few years, but I know it's going
to get better. I just pray sooner
than later. You've kept the doors
open thus far, but with our
dwindling membership and falling
behind on the rent, I don't know
how much longer we can last. Your
house is falling apart and if it's due
to my past transgressions I pray
that you don't punish your people
for my mistakes. This church needs
you right now and I know that you
are an on time God so I will leave it
all in your hands. These and all
blessings I ask in Your Son Jesus'
name, Amen."

He finishes his prayer and
turns around to see me standing in
the doorway. He looks at me a little
shocked. I guess I startled him.
After seeing the church and hearing
his prayer, I don't know if I still
want to beat him or hug him. We
stare at each a long time. He may
be wondering if I'm there to jump on
him or not. Perhaps he can see in

my eyes that Alexis told me what happened last night.

"What's going on, Sean? What brings you down here this afternoon?" He breaks the silence.

I walk into the office trying to bring my anger back to the forefront of my mind. "Actually, I wanted to talk to you about your talk with Alexis last night."

His eyes get big. He knows he should have said something last night. He probably figured since the women didn't say anything, why should he worry about it? What was said and done was said and done. "I thought that might come up."

"What's wrong with you? I try to give us a chance to have a relationship and you disrespect my woman. Then you try to demand that Andrea do what you want her to do and not what makes her happy."

"I got this from your mother last night." He says motioning for me to sit.

I sit in the chair in front of his desk. "Now you'll get it from me. Tell me what is wrong with you so that I can know whether I can continue to be in your life."

The last statement hit him pretty good. We haven't been on good terms for a while but I still talked with him and saw him every once in a while. Now he was facing not seeing me ever again. And if that happens and I have kids, he'll never see his grandchildren.

He begins by telling me he fears of losing Andrea to LA like he lost me. Andrea was the child he was able to be truly close with because there has been a barrier between the two of us for years. He also tells me that he knows Andrea can dance, but doesn't think she'll be able to make a living doing it. He goes on to say that he's scared of what the future holds for him and his church. He says that Andrea has been a bright spot in the church because of her praise dancing. If she leaves, that will be the final straw in his church going under.

"What happened to the church? You never said anything to me about it falling apart."

"It was none of your concern, Sean. You had your life to live and I didn't want to get in the way."

"But I have a little money now. I could have helped raise more to keep the maintenance up. It looks horrible down there."

"How do you think I would feel going to my son and asking for money?"

"Like a man admitting he needs help. This is crazy. You'd let your church fall apart before allowing your pride to ask for help?"

He sits back in his chair. "Would you have helped me? You barely talk to me anymore and when you do it's always cold."

I stand, knowing that I've held visual animosity towards my father for years. He hurt my mother and I have not been able to forgive him and I don't know why. My mother has forgiven him and even helped take on the responsibility of his mistake. Maybe that's a question I need to ask her and then maybe I could learn to forgive him.

"Sean." Like God had heard my thoughts, I turn around and see my mother and Alexis standing in the doorway.

"Mom, what are you doing down here with Alexis?"

Both women walk into the room. "Alexis told me you stormed out of the house and was heading down here with fire in your eyes. I guess I'm the extinguisher."

Little did she know, but the images of the church quenched my burning desire to hurt The Good Reverend Winters. I look at Alexis as she nervously stands by the door, hoping fireworks weren't about to start. I hold my hand out and she walks to me and takes it.

"I have a question for you, Mom."

"Oh Lord, let me sit down." She sits on the couch against the wall of the office where my father takes a nap sometimes.

"What made you forgive dad and stay with him all these years? Why stay if he cheated."

The Good Reverend Winters looks at her as if wanting to know the answer as much as me. My mother looks at me as if she's wondered why it took me so long to ask, or maybe it was a look of why did you ask me at all. She looks at my father and smiles, which shocks me. I would expect her to get angry when thinking of my father's affair eighteen years ago.

"Sean, it wasn't easy. It took a lot of prayer and patience, but above all else, it was God and the fact is your father has never lied. He's always been honest even when he's done wrong."

She goes on to explain how she was ready to divorce my father immediately after finding out about the affair, but when Tricia disappeared, she felt as if that part of their life was behind them and they could move on without worries. Then, when she found out about Andrea, and that Tricia died, she didn't want to help raise my father's baby. She said for weeks my father got up whenever Andrea cried in the middle of the night. He did everything for the baby without any help from her. My father was preparing sermons, making meetings, teaching Bible study and teaching at the Bible college. He would then pick Andrea up from day care or my aunt's house and bathe, feed and put Andrea down to sleep.

My mother goes on to tell us that one night when she knew my father was worn out, Andrea started crying and The Good Reverend Winters slowly started to get up, almost zombie like. My mother put her hand on his arm and told him to sleep and she would handle her. When she went into the room to get

Andrea, she held her in her arms for the first time and fell in love. She said she fed her and changed her diaper and just stared at the child who was beginning to look like her mother. She said she saw past Andrea's looks and saw her as an innocent child in need of a mother's love.

From then on, my mother began helping more and more until Andrea became more like their child than the proof of my fathers infidelity. She finally decided to adopt Andrea since she had taken on the role of mother anyway. She said it was never Andrea's fault and she never wanted to be resentful towards her. That's why she considers Andrea as much her daughter as I am her son.

"Sean, above everything, I stayed with your father because I knew that no matter what happened, he would be honest and tell me the whole truth. That's the most important thing in relationships, open and honest communication."

The Good Reverend Winters chimes in. "That's true, Sean. Open communication brings total honesty and honesty brings trust. I made a mistake and paid for it. I had another mouth to feed and send through school. I also lost church members and respect in the community. As you can see, the church house has suffered as well."

"Communication, honesty and trust kept you guys together?" Alexis asks still holding my hand.

My mother nods. "Yes, and our faith helped us weather that storm and all others."

I look to my father, finally seeing him as a good responsible man and not just a preacher who had an affair. He's a man who made a mistake and he's not the only one. Even though he's a preacher, he still has a sin nature like all of us. He's basically a sheep himself. It's just he's been called by God to lead the sheep. I understand him more because I'm having the same issues right now, having two different women at once.

I look at my watch. "I have to get Alexis over to Natalie's store, but Dad, we need to talk about how we're going to fix this church up and get it back to what it used to be."

He smiles and nods at me in agreement. I walk to my mom and kiss her on the cheek and thank

311

her. She hugs me tight and gives me a kiss on the cheek as well. I look at Alexis and smile. I take her by the hand and lead her out of the church and down the street to my parents' place. She runs into the house to grab some make-up and a change of clothes.

I look across the street and see Summer's car is gone. I think about what my mother said about staying with my father and having open communication. I think about what happened between Summer and me this morning and how much I hurt Alexis because of it. Even though I didn't sleep with Summer, the sting of my desire was enough to hurt Alexis. It made me not want to put myself in that situation again. So I have decided that I'm done with Summer and that I only need Alexis. But man, it would have been good to sleep with Summer one more time.

Chapter 22

Summer

I stand in Natalie's office wearing a beautiful green and brown evening gown. I remember Natalie using me as a model a year ago when she designed this dress. This was the only dress I wanted to wear tonight, even though there are two different outfits Natalie wants me to wear for the grand opening. I think back to all the times I've modeled for Natalie. Ever since we were teenagers Natalie has used me as her live mannequin.

I was actually excited about modeling for Natalie tonight, that is, until I found out Natalie had become buddy-buddy with Alexis. Ever since I arrived at the store an hour ago all Natalie has been talking about is how great it was going to be to have a professional model her clothes. She also talked Sean into taking some pictures, which he may be able to sell to a magazine or something. Natalie had a little power couple making all her dreams come true.

I stand and stare into the full-length mirror on Natalie's wall next to her desk. I love the way I look in this dress. I love the soft fabric on my skin. The dress hugs all my curves. The green and brown heels make my ass sit up nice. I really feel like a princess. Now all I need is my prince, Prince Sean, by my side and all will be right with my kingdom.

Suddenly, Natalie bursts into the office looking stressed but smiling. "There you are girl. Why aren't you in the dressing room changing with the other girls?"

I shoot Natalie an angry look. "I don't want to change in the room with The Model."

Natalie closes the door. "Quit tripping. She ain't even here yet." Natalie walks in front of me and my reflection in the mirror. "Now I told you and you promised not to start no drama tonight. We open in one hour and I want it to go off with out any problems or I'm going to kill you."

The last statement wasn't true, but I know Natalie would be highly upset if her opening night was ruined. And if I were the reason it was ruined, Natalie would probably kick my ass all the way to Texas. She need not worry though. I have no intention in causing a scene tonight. However, if all goes right, I will be leaving with Sean and Alexis will be on her way back to LA alone.

I have it all worked out. It is the perfect plan and I plan on executing it with precision. I am on a mission tonight and no one is going to stand in my way; no one is going to stop me from getting what I want. Sean has always been my man. I just never saw it before. But now that I know what I want, and that is Sean all to myself. I have nothing personally against Alexis as a person, but when it comes to Sean, Alexis is the enemy.

"Summer go get ready. I need you guys in place." Natalie says as she tries to gently push me to the door.

"Alright, fine. I'll go put on my make-up."

I leave Natalie's office and walk down the hallway to the private dressing room which is actually the employee break room. At the moment it's empty. The other two girls must have walked out into the store or went to the rest room. The dressing/break room is small. No privacy from the other's in the room. It has a small table sitting in front of a mirror where I sit and begin applying my make-up. Just as I finish putting on my earth tone lip stick, Alexis walks in, stops and stares at me for a second before putting her things down on a round table in the middle of the room.

"Hi, Alexis," I say with fake enthusiasm.

"Summer," Alexis, says trying to be cordial but not friendly.

Alexis begins pulling out her make-up and avoids eye contact with me. I apply green eye shadow, trying to match my beautiful gown. For a moment I catch myself staring at Alexis. She's so beautiful it's sickening. Flawless skin, small but full lips, perfect thin nose and gorgeous light brown eyes. The only things I have that are better are my ass and tits. Her thin ass is no match for my juicy booty and C-cup breasts.

Before I can take my eyes off my nemesis, she catches me staring at her. She doesn't say anything, but her silence is speaking loud and clear. She's about to let what little street she has come out. She doesn't take her eyes off of me. Finally, I let out a little giggle and turn my attention back to my make-up. I decide that now it's time to put the next phase of "Operation Get Sean Back" into action.

"Does Sean still do that lick then suck, lick then suck motion I taught him?" I ask with out looking at her.

"Summer, don't start. You can stop with the fakeness around me. I get enough of that in Los Angeles. You don't have to like me, but you should know I'm going to be around for a long time."

I turn to face Alexis. "Excuse the hell out of me! I was just trying to make sure a sista was getting it right."

"I'm wearing the ring. I'm getting it right and he must be too to wife me." Alexis shoots back.

I just smile. I got under Alexis' skin, which is exactly what I wanted to do. Now it was time to go in for the kill. "So when Sean kissed you, how did I taste?"

Alexis drops her make-up and starts to walk towards me, but stops when Natalie and the other two young models walk into the dressing room.

"Alright ladies, we're about to open the store so lets go over your roles for tonight." Natalie says in an excited yet nervous voice.

Alexis walks to the other side of the round table and sits with her back to me. I can tell she's pissed and that makes me happy. The other two girls sit in the two chairs next to Alexis. Natalie doesn't sit. She seems too nervous to sit or even stand still.

"Alright ladies, we have less than an hour before the doors open." Natalie begins. "So, you know that you all have three outfit changes, first the evening gowns, then the 'N' jeans and T-shirts and finally the lingerie."

Natalie goes on to explain the purpose of each outfit and why she's going in the order she's going. Basically, she wants to show her elegant side first because that's what she's known for. The Jeans and T-shirts are to show that she's still down with the everyday female who wants to dress down but still

318

look cute. The lingerie is for the men as much as it's for the women, and it's Natalie's newest venture. She just started designing teddy's, mini dresses and garters this past year. A few discreet clients have asked her to design something sexy for their husbands or boyfriends. It turns out lingerie may be her biggest seller.

"Any questions ladies?" Natalie asks at the end of her speech.

No one has any questions. The other two girls and I were already in their gowns but Alexis had just gotten there and wasn't ready. Natalie shows Alexis her dress. I watch as Alexis puts on a purple dress that has one of the shoulders out. I have to admit, Alexis looks good in the dress. It hugs her curves perfectly; her arms and legs are well toned and even have a beautiful glow. When she puts on the purple heels Natalie picked out, they show off her sexy calf's and make her butt stand at attention. Heels and form fitting clothes tend to help women with little booties like Alexis.

I begin to feel myself become jealous, but I have to stay on mission. I know I have Alexis flustered and now I've put the idea in her head that Sean and I had sex, even if Sean told her we didn't. It will make the next move perfect, but the next move will have to wait a while. First I need to get through Natalie's grand opening with no problems.

Alexis puts on her make up with a small compact she has in her make-up bag. Natalie tells us all to get into place. Alexis and the two girls follow Natalie out the room to get into place. I wait until they walk out then I make my way over to Alexis's purse that's sitting on the table. I open it and pull out Alexis' cell phone. I take the phone to my purse on the table where I was doing my make-up. I place the phone in my purse and look in the mirror and smile.

Natalie walks back in. "Summer, will you come on!"

I blow myself a kiss in the mirror and turn and walk out the room with Natalie. I look good and feel good. My plan is working out perfectly. If it keeps going the way it's supposed to, Sean will be snatching that ring off of Alexis' finger and putting it on mine. Phase one, two and three have already

been executed. Not it's time for the
fourth and final phase. Phase four
ends with Sean making love to me
tonight, in the morning and for the
rest of our lives.

Chapter 23

Sean

I snapped pictures of the guests, the models, Natalie and her husband Charles all evening. I haven't worked this hard since the last wedding I did a month ago and I'm not even getting paid for this. Since Natalie is my friend and has done a lot for me over the years, the least I can do is make her night as memorable as possible. I snap shots that will bring back memories of all the laughs, joy and excitement. I capture several special moments in time. They say we don't have a time machine, but photos take us back in time whenever we look at them.

And to think, I almost forgot my camera at my parents' place. I was in such deep thought I didn't think to go inside to get my camera bag. Alexis and I were in the car halfway to the store when she asked me if I put my camera in the car. I had to turn around and go back to my parents' place to get it. Then I got into a conversation with Summer's mom who was sitting on her porch drinking what she said was lemonade. The lemonade seemed to make her a little too happy. By the time I got to the store, Alexis was late and it was all my fault. I apologized to Natalie, but she didn't seem to care. She was just glad Alexis agreed to model for her.

As I snap shots of Natalie's models, I can't help but take more of Alexis than any others. Summer had her fair share of photo time as well, but I think subconsciously I was trying to avoid Summer. I wanted to focus on Alexis, my fiancée, the woman I plan to marry. I have to admit, I've been nervous all night because I thought Summer would say something or Alexis may get mad and the two might start fighting. But the night has been peaceful and civil.

The grand opening seems to be a huge success for Natalie and I'm very proud of my friend. Several customers have bought gowns and some have bought jeans. Natalie

has sent the girls back to change
into their last outfits for the evening.
I take a break and walk over to the
bar where Eric is serving up wine
and champagne for Natalie's
customers and guests.

"What up, Family? You come
for some champagne or wine?"

"I came to ask why you left me
stranded earlier?" I had not yet had
the chance to talk with him about
that whole situation and what
happened when I went into
Summer's condo.

Eric smiles at me, knowing he
was wrong, but thought he was
doing what I wanted him to do. "I
figured you were going to be a
while."

"Come on, Eric, you know I'm
about to get married man, that's not
cool. You set me up for failure."

"Dude, you set yourself up for
failure by going over there. Plus you
told me to go anyway."

I look at Eric for a second
trying to figure out where he
remembered me telling him to leave.
I told him to stay, so what happened
wouldn't happen. I know I didn't
tell him to leave, but he seems to
think I did.

"Eric, I didn't tell you to leave."

Eric pulls out his cell phone and goes to a text message and hands me the phone. I see that the text is from Summer and it says: Eric, Sean says to come back in a while, he'll text you when he's ready to leave.

I hand the phone back to Eric. "I never told her to send you a text."

Krystal walks over to us. I give her a quick belly rub. I know that must drive pregnant women crazy, but I just can't help it. I look at her finger and see that the ring Eric had earlier is now placed prominently on her Krystal's ring finger. I grab her hand and look at the ring. I give her another hug and congratulate her. I turn to Eric and shake his hand.

"I didn't know it went down already." I'm guessing he went home and asked her after he left me.

"Man, Family, when you didn't call me back earlier I had extra time on my hands and just decided to go for it."

"I told him no at first." Krystal says with a light giggle. "I thought he had done something wrong."

"Yeah and I told her I was finally doing something right." Eric says as he grabs a glass and takes a sip of the champagne he's supposed to be serving.

"Well, I'm happy for you guys."

"We're happy for you." Krystal says. "And I'm sorry if I said too much earlier. You know how I get to talking." She walks to Eric who puts his free arm around her and kisses her on the forehead.

I tell Krystal I forgive her and that it wasn't a big deal. Then I see Alexis, Summer and the other models come from the back office area in some sexy lingerie. I couldn't help but stare. I turn my camera on and speed walk towards the models. I begin to snap shots of the women as they pose for the customers, guests and me. Other folks have taken out their phones and are taking photos too. Natalie has security quickly make them put their phones away.

Alexis smiles for my camera. I can tell she's getting turned on. She has been since I started snapping pictures of her when the store first opened. Not to mention the fact that Eric has supplied her with two glasses of champagne during her wardrobe changes. She wears an orange teddy and matching panties with orange and white heels. As I watch Alexis in her lingerie, I think about taking her to one of the back rooms and giving her the best of me. I try to stay in work mode but it's hard, very hard when Alexis is standing there looking edible.

I try to divert my attention and take pictures of the other models. Summer looks good in an all white mini dress and white heels. She blows a kiss. I'm not sure if it's for the camera or me. More than likely it was for me, but I'm moving on. I have a good woman that I don't want to hurt. I continue to snap for a few more minutes then turn my attention to the customers who are all in the lingerie section trying to find the perfect set for their men.

After about ten minutes, Natalie allows the girls to go to the back and change into their regular clothes. Natalie planned to keep the store opened for another two or three hours but she didn't want the models to freeze in their lingerie.

I walk to Natalie who stands towards the front of the store taking pictures with customers and guests. Charles stands off to the side. I walk to him and shake his hand.

"She finally did it." I tell him.

"Yeah, she's finally got it opened."

"So does that mean you get your house back? I know she's moved all of those mannequins and sewing machines out."

"Man, no. She still designs at home, but she promised to spend more time working here and not at home. Do you know how hard it is to watch a football game while she's sewing something?" He says shaking his head.

I know Charles didn't mind too much. He was drunk in love with Natalie. From the first time he asked her to dance at a club seven years ago, he was in love. He gave her some corny line, but Natalie thought he was handsome and she agreed to dance with him. After the club they talked for a while outside then exchanged numbers and continued to talk over the phone. Finally, Natalie agreed to go out with him and within four months she was talking marriage, although the wedding didn't happen for another two years. They've been married the last four or so years and seem to have it all together.

"So, what's marriage like?" I mean you two seem to be happy."

Charles looks at me in the eye. "It's like completion. You know how you can have everything going your way, but still feel like you haven't got the one thing you need to make it complete. When I married Natalie, I felt complete."

I give him dap. "That was deep."

"That was truth," he says as Natalie walks over to him and kisses him and then hugs me.

"Sean, thank you so much for taking pictures tonight. I really appreciate it," she says.

"No problem."

I feel my cell phone vibrate. I pull it out and see I have a text from Alexis: Meet me in the break room." I smile. I turned her on out here when I was taking pictures of her. Now it's time for me to turn her out in the break room. I tell Natalie and Charles I'm going to go to the rest room. I give my camera to Eric to watch for a few minutes. I walk to the back, shaking hands with a few customers of whom I took pictures during the evening.

I walk to the break room, but the door is closed and locked so I knock twice. The door suddenly opens and I walk in. I don't see anyone at first, but then the door closes behind me. I turn around to see Summer standing at the door wearing nothing but the white heels, her body oiled up and shining

"Summer, what the hell?" I scream as she starts to walk towards me.

"We didn't get to finish what we started earlier at my place."

I back up trying to distance myself from Summer. I don't see the chair behind me and I trip and fall to the ground. Before I can get up, Summer is on top of me, kissing me. I try to get her off, but I can't get a grip on her oily body.

"Stop fighting it, Sean. You know you still want me. Once you taste this sweetness again, you'll remember."

Suddenly, and before I can do anything about it, Summer straddles my face. I inhale her as she slowly grinds her lips on my nose and lips. "Summer stop." She doesn't. She has my face on her lips and is trying to get me to taste her. A piece of me wants to give in and kiss her lips, but I know I can't. I made a promise to Alexis and to myself.

The next thing I know the door opens and Summer jumps up quickly looking for something to cover herself with. I wipe my face and sit up and look at my future walk away. Alexis just saw me face first in Summer. How am I going to explain that? I get up as Summer puts on the skirt and shirt she had on earlier today.

"What the hell were you thinking, Summer? Why would you do that?"

"I was thinking, that if we did it, you would remember how good it was. How we used to be, before Alexis."

I get angry but try and keep my voice down. "Summer, it used to be because it's in the past. I wanted only you for years, but you just never wanted me. Now that I have someone who wants me as much as I want them, you decide you want me? It's too late. I tried to see if there was something between us, but all there was is sexual attraction. Alexis is the one I want to be with, not you. You waited too long to show me you loved me. Alexis showed me first."

I walk out of the room leaving Summer standing there alone and heartbroken. I hope she doesn't cry, but right now she's not my concern. I need to find Alexis and tell her what happened. I walk out to the store and see no sign of her. I walk over to Eric ask him if he has seen Alexis.   All he does is hand me her engagement ring.

"Where did she go, Eric?"

"She just asked Krystal to take her to the airport." He tells me. "What happened? You two have a fight?"

"Finish taking photos with the camera. I gotta go get her."

I run out the store hearing Eric say something smart but not really caring. I need to find Alexis. I need to make it right.

Chapter 24

Alexis

Krystal pulls her Nissan Murano in front of Sean's parents' house and puts it in park. I sit in the passenger seat wiping tears from my eyes, even though they keep falling. I can't believe I just caught Sean cheating on me. After all of his talk about how he only wanted to be with me, he ends up being like all the other men in my life. I forgave him for his slip earlier because I felt I had part to play in the situation. He promised me that she was out of his system as we drove to Natalie's store. I see that was all a lie. Summer flat out told me Sean went down on her earlier. I tried to ignore it, but after what I just saw, I can see she's telling the truth.

I try to regain my composure and not make such a scene in front of Krystal. "Thank you for the ride, Krystal."

Krystal has a look of concern on her face. From what Sean has told me, she's been in my shoes before. "No problem, girl."

I reach for the door to open it, but Krystal puts her hand on my arm. I turn to face her trying to fight back tears. Krystal opens her arms wide and I go in for a hug. It was a difficult hug because of Krystal's expecting tummy, but it made me feel a little better.

"Don't worry, Alexis, everything is going to be alright." Krystal says with all sincerity

I break the hug and smile at Krystal. I believe the two of us could have been good friends. I get out of the car and walk to the house. Krystal drives off when I get to the downstairs apartment door. At first I wanted Krystal to drive me to the airport, but I didn't want to be rude and make her miss the rest of the grand opening. So I just asked her for a ride to Sean's parents' place and I would call a taxi when I was done packing.

Toni had given Sean and me each a key to the downstairs apartment so we would have access when she or her husband weren't home, which they weren't at the moment. I walk in and turn on a light. I walk to the closet and grab my suitcase and begin packing with tears still streaming down my face. The image of Summer on top of Sean naked and riding his face turned my stomach. I feel my heart beating faster as I imagine what they had done earlier in the day when Sean said they only kissed. Was he lying? Had there been more? Have they been doing it since we arrived in town?

I can't do it anymore. I need someone to calm me down a little. I pull out my cell phone and call Simone. Simone answers on the second ring and I go right into the story before she can even get a word out. I tell Simone about Summer and how she was Sean's first love. I tell her about my anxiety about seeing Summer in person and what would happen if she and Sean were alone. I tell her about the first meeting at Natalie's store and the wink. I tell her about the admission of the kiss. I then tell her about catching Summer on top of Sean less than an hour ago.

"Damn, girl. What you going to do?" Simone asks when I finish giving her the rundown.

"I'm coming home. I'm going to move my stuff out of the Condo and I guess I'm sleeping in your guest bedroom until I find me a place."

"Lexis, you know I turned that guest bedroom into my office."

"Well, I'm sleeping on the couch!" I yell.

"Hold on with the tone. And are you sure you're not jumping the gun?" Simone asks.

My voice stays elevated. "He was eating her out on the break room floor. What would you do?"

"Probably kick his ass. But in your case, I would talk to him first because you don't know what really went on."

"Well, he didn't come out to talk to me so I guess he stayed and enjoyed himself."

Simone knows all about my past boyfriends, even the drug dealer who got my little brother locked up. "I'm just saying that I know Sean and he loves you. The way he looks at you tells me that you are the only one he wants to be with. If you ask me, I say something doesn't seem right."

"I guess neither of us knew
Sean as well as we thought. In the
end, he's just like all the rest. I'm
done with men for good. From now
on it's just me and God."

"Come on now. You can't stay
away from the magic stick anymore
than I can," Simone says.

"Watch me. I'm going to be
celibate for the rest of my life." I
even had to laugh a little at my
declaration.

Simone laughed a little as well.
"All I'm saying, Cuz, is talk to him
first. Sean's a good man. You don't
want to lose that. Do you?"

"He got his ring back. Enough
said," I tell her as I finish packing
the suitcase.

"Well if that's what you want,
Cuz, I have your back. I just think
it's a mistake," Simone tells me.

"Girl, just pick me up from Bob
Hope International in a few hours.
I'll call you when I land."

"Okay, Lexis."

I hang up with Simone and do
a Goggle search on my phone to find
a taxi service. I find one and make
the call to have one pick me up and
take me to the airport. I place the
key on the card table in the small
kitchen area and walk out of the

small apartment locking the bottom
lock on my way out. I walk to the
sidewalk and wait for my taxi, which
should be arriving within fifteen
minutes. I look at my empty ring
finger and begin to tear up again,
but I don't let them fall. I'm done
crying. A cheater like Sean doesn't
deserve my tears. I begin to pray
that God help me get though this
heartache and pain I'm feeling right
now.

Chapter 25

Sean

I'm pissed because I was speeding towards the airport trying to catch Alexis before she left for Los Angeles. Then I get a text from Eric that said Krystal was back at Natalie's store and Alexis was at my parents' place packing. He also said Alexis was going to get a taxi to take her to the airport. I get off I 580 East and hop on I 580 West trying to get to my parents' place before Alexis leaves.

I pull in front of my parents' place and see Alexis standing on the curb, still waiting for a taxi. I put the car in park but don't turn off the engine. I hop out and run to her. She tries to back away from me when I try to hug her. I have a chance to make this right and I'm not going to waste it.

"Sean, I don't want to talk to you," she says trying to avoid eye contact with me.

"Baby, you have to believe me. I didn't do anything wrong."

Alexis finally looks me in the eyes. I see the rage in hers. Before I can do or say anything else, she slaps me across the face.

"You didn't do anything wrong? You had a naked woman on your face!" Alexis yells as tears form in her already red and puffy eyes.

"I was set up, Alexis. From the very beginning I was set up."

I figured it all out when I saw Eric's text message from Summer. Summer had it planned from the beginning. She called me the other night because she knew I would be intrigued by her needing to talk to me. She knew that if she seemed hurt at the mall yesterday, that I would try and make it right by coming to her house and finishing our talk. She knew that I would stop her this morning and she made sure she dropped me off in front of Alexis where everyone could see. She took Alexis' phone and text me to meet her in the dressing room and then got me caught up in what seemed like us having sex. Summer always gets what she wants, but I've never seen her go to such extraordinary measures to do so.

"Men are always set up when they get caught doing wrong" Alexis says as her taxi pulls in front of the house and parks. She walks past me to the taxi driver, who has gotten out of the car. He takes her suitcase and puts it in the trunk. "I'll leave the key to the condo under the mat."

I run to Alexis and stop her from getting into the taxi. She tries to wrestle out my grip, but I'm too strong for her. She bites my hand which makes me release one hand. She then slaps me again and starts hitting me in my face, arms and chest. I grab her arms and restrain her. The taxi driver comes towards me to intervene. I give him a look that makes him back down. He gets into his cab and gets on the phone, probably calling the police.

"Alexis just listen to me."

"No!" She screams still trying to get away from me.

"She lied to Eric this morning."

Alexis finally stops trying to fight me seeing she can't win.

"Baby, she set me up from the beginning."

I tell Alexis about the text Summer sent to Eric this morning and how I got a text to meet her, not Summer, in the dressing room. Alexis doesn't believe me at first, but I tell her to look at her phone. She pulls out her phone, but there is no text sent to me in her history. She tries again to get into the taxi. I hold her with one arm and pull out my cell phone and show her the text requesting that I come to the break room. Reading the text, Alexis sees that the text is from her phone.

Alexis goes from hurt to furious. "I'm going to kick her ass! No, I'm going to kill her!" □ "No need, Baby. I'm still here with you. You're the one I want to be with."

"But she was on top of you and you were... You had your face in her...."

I tell Alexis the whole story and how I tripped and before I could get up Summer was on top of me. I told her how Summer got up after she walked and in and saw us. I tell her that Summer just wanted to have sex with me and that hopefully it would make me fall in love with her again. I told Summer it was too late and that I only wanted to be with her.

342

Alexis smiles and kisses me. "I'm sorry, I shouldn't have hit you."

"It's okay. I just want us to be alright."

"If you're willing to give me my ring back then we will be."

"Only if you promise not to take it off again."

Alexis kisses me again. "I promise."

I take the ring out of my pants pocket and place it back on her finger. I kiss her and hug her tight. I tell the taxi driver to take the suitcase out of the trunk and have him call off the police. He tells me he didn't call the cops. He called his wife to check on the kids. He says this wasn't the first time he's seen a couple fight. I give him thirty bucks and he drives off. Alexis and I stand on the curb. I hug her and kiss her again, happy that I didn't lose her.

"So does this mean she's truly out of your system?" Alexis asks.

I nod. "Summer is out of my system for good. You don't have to worry about Summer ever again."

Chapter 26

Summer

I sit in the back of Fellowship Baptist Church. I arrived late to the church Anniversary service and had gone unnoticed by everyone. It is packed with members of other churches in attendance. I wasn't as worried about the service as I was about the outcome of my plan to get Sean. I expected Alexis to leave town last night and Sean would run to me for comfort, but it never happened.

I listened to the end of Reverend Winters' sermon on forgiveness. Sean called me last night and apologized for how he talked to me at Natalie's store. I thought it was the opening to him professing his love, but instead he told me he only wanted to be with Alexis. I was crushed but didn't feel defeated. After a few drinks, I renewed my faith to make Sean mine. I just need Alexis out of the way. She doesn't deserve him. Alexis can't love Sean the way I do and soon he'll find out she's not the one for him.

Reverend Winters made a special announcement that Sean was engaged. Everyone clapped expect me. Sean and Alexis stand and wave to everyone, full of smiles. Reverend Winters goes on to announce that Sean would help re-build the church and bring it back to life. This brought more applause. Sean already put up twenty thousand dollars for remodeling. Reverend Winters also says that Sean will be raising more money in the coming months.

The next announcement is about Andrea, who is set to start school at San Francisco State and double majoring in Dance and Business. This brought even more applause as Andrea, who is seated in the front row with her mother stands and waves. I find it odd that the Winters family seems so happy so soon. I know all about Sean and Reverend Winters dislike for each other. And since when did Reverend Winters become a man that sends his daughter to dancing school? It's just not his style.

I start to think about how I'll get Sean back. The only problem is Alexis. I need to find a way to make Sean see that Alexis isn't the perfect little woman. The problem is that she seems like the perfect woman. But everyone has something; everyone has skeletons in their closet. I am going to find Alexis' deep, dark secret. There has to be some dirt on Alexis out there and I'm going to be the one to expose it. By the time I'm done, Alexis will regret the day she stepped foot in Sean's studio and stole him from me. Alexis doesn't know who the hell she just pissed off. Summer Boyd wasn't the one to play with. Alexis just started a war of the hearts. She may have won this battle, but she won't win the war.

The service ends and people exit the sanctuary. I get up first and walk out trying to avoid being seen. I quickly walk through the lobby and towards the exit door. A church member who knows my mother stops me. We make small talk for a moment. As the woman says goodbye, I look to the lobby and make eye contact with Alexis who is standing with Sean, but he is looking in the opposite direction. Alexis' smiling face turns to a frown as she stares at me. I smile and wink at her then exit the church.

I walk to my BMW and get in. I check my make-up in the visor mirror. I smile at my reflection, thinking to myself, "How can Sean not want me?" My first plan to get Sean back failed, but I always get what I want. I don't know the date for Sean's wedding, but I plan for them not to make it to the alter. Sean is mine and no little model is going to take him away from me. He is just confused right now and Alexis has him not thinking straight. She's got him brain washed.

"So what is my next move?" Whatever it is it has to be big so that Sean knows that I really want to be with him and only him. I think about a question my little sister, Nicole, asked me a few years back. "What do you do when the one you love doesn't love you back?" My answer was, "Make them love you." And that's what I plan to do. I am going to make Sean love me.

DISCLAIMER

The church used in this novel is a work of fiction. Though there is a church on the corner of 44th Street and Linden in North Oakland it is not the church in this novel. Also the homes of The Good Reverend Winters, Summer's parents' and Summer's condo, Sean's studio and condo are all fictitious. Natalie's store is also a work of fiction.

BOOK CLUB QUESTIONS

1. Do you believe Sean made the right choice in staying with Alexis?
2. What could Summer have done differently to get Sean back?
3. Do believe Sean cheated on Alexis when he kissed Summer?
4. Is having an emotional love affair worse than having a physical affair?
5. Do you think Sean still loves Summer?
6. Do you believe Summer really loved Sean?
7. Should Alexis have told Sean to confront his feelings for Summer?
8. Do you believe Alexis is a hypocrite because off of her profession? She loves God, but she poses half naked is magazines and videos. Even though it's stated her work is tasteful, is she sending a bad message to young Christian women?
9. Do you believe that Sean was ever in control with his relationship with Summer?

10. Do you believe Sean was wrong for holding a grudge against The Good Reverend Winters for his past infidelity?

11. Do you believe The Good Reverend Winters deserved forgiveness from Sean? From Toni? From his congregation?

12. Would you take care of you husbands out-of-wedlock child?

13. Do you believe Toni to be weak strong?

14. What are the similarities between Alexis and Summer? What are their differences?

15. What is Sean's attraction Summer? To Alexis?

ACKNOWLEDGEMENTS

I thank God forgiving me the gift of
writing. I thank God for giving me
the idea of Winters' Summer as I
flew home from a visit to LA ten
years ago. I thank God for guiding
me on this journey of life. I have
been blessed beyond what I deserve.
If you have not yet accepted Jesus
as your personal Lord and Savior I
urge you to do so. I am not a
perfect man nor do I pretend to be.
What I am is a sinner saved by
grace. Grace and mercy are free
gifts from God. For God so loved the
world that He sent His only begotten
son Jesus to die for the worlds sins
John 3:16. We didn't do anything to
deserve it. All we have to do is
accept it. To me it's simple. Accept
the free gift of Grace and have
eternal life in heaven. I have my
ticket to Glory I urge you to get
yours.
To my wife Nasinet (Nasa) I love you
so much. I appreciate you for

always having my back and supporting me. Thank you for taking the kids out of the house and giving me hours to focus on my writing. Thank you for being my toughest critic and my best friend. I LOVE YOU.

I thank my kids Bryan and Menah because you guys taught me patience and helped me to stop procrastinating and making excuses for why I'm not writing. You don't know it but you two made me grow up and get my priorities straight.

I thank my parents Ellis and Stephanie Jackson. My parents are the most supportive parents in the world. I love you guys. You have banked rolled all of my projects so this book is as much yours as it's mine.

I thank my brother Marcus Jackson for always showing support. If it wasn't mom and dad you were bank rolling me and I appreciate it.

I thank my grandmother Helen Woods who helped raise and shape me. I love you.

I thank my God Parents Fred and Cynthia. You two have all given me words of wisdom and encouragement over the years.

Though we don't see much of each other nowadays I want you both to know I love you and appreciate you.

I want to thank my editors/proofreaders and cousins Ronald Jackson II and D'Ouita Woods. You helped mold this manuscript into a great story.
I have to thank all my Uncles, Aunts and Cousins who have supported me over the years. Here goes and I pray I hope don't forget anybody: Uncle Ron and Auntie Jan, Uncle Rick and Auntie Ella, Auntie Kathy and Uncle Clyde, Uncle Ken, Jason, Chelia, Brigee, Shavaki, Andre, Theresa (French Fri.), Kim Richardson, Hana Coleman, Danielle, Asokah, Auntie Bette, Aunt Lynn, Shonda, Charles Jackson and Norma, Charles (LA), Carlos, Bobbie, Carmen, Bonnie, Cookie, Exzetta, Art, Eric and Ron, Donnie, and Jessica. If I missed anyone charge it to my head and not my heart.
I want to thank my friends and supporters: Tyjun, Antrina, Ben, Valerie Patton, Arthur Young, Christina and Mike Glendinning, Kay-c, De Young, Mieko, Joy Morgan, Darrin Hodges, Darrin and Lori Baker, James and Loni Battle,

Joan Leadbetter, Diana and Steve
McCarter, Denise Tracy, Dave
Gregory, Angel, Jahi and Lori,
Terrence (K. C.), Lisa Luttinger,
Jovan and Kelly (Nikki B).
Special thanks to David and Lyn
Talbert. David, you told me to keep
writing and I haven't stopped since.
Special thanks to Mary "Honey B"
Morrison. You have given me
priceless advice. I appreciate it.
Special thanks to authors Kimberla
Lawson Roby and Lutisha Lovely. I
haven't met you in person but our e-
mails have given lots of advice.
I want to thank all of my co-workers
at the Kaiser Permanente Optical
Lab who came out to my plays and
have supported me in my writing
career. Especially everyone in the
administration office who kept
encouraging me to keep writing.
I want to give special thanks to
Pastor Donel Reedus, First Lady
Judy Reedus and the entire East
Bay Bible Church family. I love you
all and appreciate all of the support
over the years. If you're looking for
a church home please visit
eastbaybiblechurch.com. Also
check us out on the radio KFAX
1100-AM Sundays at 3 pm. Yes,
that was a commercial.

I also want to thank Pastor Allen
Barns and the Community Baptist
Church family. Community is
where I first accepted Jesus as my
Lord and Savior. Though I don't get
to see the members much I want
you to know there is no loss of love
or respect for my original church
family.
I also want to acknowledge those
who are no longer here but left me
with words of wisdom. May you rest
in peace. Ellis Jackson (Grandpa
Jack), Henry Woods (Grandpa
Woody), Ruth Mary Jackson
(Grandma Ruth), Barbra Bailey,
Uncle Earl, Aunt Georgia Lee
Sexton, Aunt Stella and Aunt Ruby.

COMING SOON !!!!!!!!

Sonny Knights

ABOUT THE AUTHOR

D. Lamar Jackson was born and
raised in Oakland, California. He is
a graduate of San Francisco State
University. He has written several
stage plays as well as the novella
Lilies in Spring. He is the editor and
chief of D. Lamar Ink, llc. Winters'
Summer is the first novel under this
imprint. The next novel Sonny
Knights is scheduled for a 2013
release. D. Lamar still resides in the
Bay Area with his wife and two
children. For all news, info and
updates visit www.dlamarink.com or
follow him on Twitter
@dlamarthewriter or on Facebook
under the handle D. Lamar
Jackson.